"JOLIE, WHEN CAN I SEE YOU AGAIN?"

She shook her head. "Morgan—"

"And I mean on a *real* date. Tonight was not a genuine representation of what I have to offer. Although it did have its moments."

"Tonight was . . . tonight was nice, but . . ." her voice trailed away.

"But?"

"I'm not looking for love, and I'm not interested in fooling around." She kissed her fingertips and touched his lips gently. "Good night, Morgan."

"Is that it?"

"Isn't that the way friends say good night?"

Caressing her with his eyes, Morgan longed to take her into his arms and kiss her the way she needed to be kissed. "I can be patient," he warned. "But I think you and I both know that we are destined for more than friendship."

CANDLELIGHT ECSTASY CLASSIC ROMANCES

CANDLELIGHT ECSTASY ROMANCES®

ONCE UPON A DREAM

JoAnn Stacey

A CANDLELIGHT ECSTASY ROMANCE®

Published by
Dell Publishing Co., Inc.
1 Dag Hammarskjold Plaza
New York, New York 10017

Dell ® TM 681510, Dell Publishing Co., Inc.

Candlelight Ecstasy Romance®, 1,203,540, is a registered
trademark of Dell Publishing Co., Inc., New York, New York.

ISBN: 0-440-16722-1

Printed in the United States of America

May 1987

10 9 8 7 6 5 4 3 2 1

WFH

To Our Readers:

We have been delighted with your enthusiastic response to Candlelight Ecstasy Romances®, and we thank you for the interest you have shown in this exciting series.

In the upcoming months we will continue to present the distinctive sensuous love stories you have come to expect only from Ecstasy. We look forward to bringing you many more books from your favorite authors and also the very finest work from new authors of contemporary romantic fiction.

As always, we are striving to present the unique, absorbing love stories that you enjoy most—books that are more than ordinary romance. Your suggestions and comments are always welcome. Please write to us at the address below.

Sincerely,

The Editors
Candlelight Romances
1 Dag Hammarskjold Plaza
New York, New York 10017

ONCE UPON A DREAM

CHAPTER ONE

"That one could slay dragons under my bed anytime."

Jolie O'Day grimaced at the rapturous expression on her friend's face. "Sharon, how many times do I have to tell you? We're here to sell food, not to ogle the innocent bystanders." She went back to arranging delicate wedges of quiche on the lavender foil plates that were a trademark of their tearoom, Quiche and Tell.

"Oh, yeah, I keep forgetting." Sharon Connelly made no move to get back to work and continued gazing into the colorfully costumed crowd. "But that bystander was born to be ogled and I sincerely doubt his innocence," the buxom redhead said, propping her chin on her palms. "Come on, Jolie, just because you've sworn off men until you reach menopause doesn't mean you can't at least look."

"Why window-shop when you aren't in the market to buy?" Jolie shrugged her slim shoulders. In her limited experience, relationships with men were what women had when they didn't know better.

"Really, Jolie!" Sharon frowned at her best friend. "Sometimes I truly believe you're hopeless."

Jolie's smile was bittersweet. That wasn't entirely true. She had so many hopes, so many dreams. However, none of them involved men.

Jolie thanked her customer and straightened her tall, cone-shape headdress, pulling the flowing purple chiffon scarf and a strand of her lustrous dark hair away from her eyes. A gust of wind played with her hair and flapped the banners that popped overhead. The noisily fluttering flags and streamers were only a small part of the cacophony of sounds at the Medieval Fair.

Nearby, ducks quacked and squabbled over popcorn and crumbs tossed into the duck pond by generous fairgoers. A piper in a Pan costume skipped past, a group of romping children trailing in his wake. Across the way the voices of a madrigal group rose harmoniously on a balmy April breeze. Jolie breathed deeply of air so clean and green it could almost be tasted. It was a perfect Oklahoma spring day.

In the past four years she'd grown ever more conscious of the sounds that filled her life—sounds most people took for granted. Sounds her daughter would never hear. She gazed lovingly at Meggie's small, dear face.

The child's bright fawn-brown eyes didn't miss a thing as she peered into the crowd from atop an overturned crate. She rested her dimpled chin on her palms, mimicking Sharon's pose. Meggie looked like a woodland sprite in the green pixie costume Jolie had made for her, and the gay wreath of silk flowers on her head was a bright contrast to her shiny brown curls.

Meggie was a joy to Jolie, the best part of a life that had never been great. Sweet-tempered and loving, she was locked in a world without sound.

"There he is again," Sharon said, a heartfelt sigh tacked on at the end of her observation. "Isn't he the most impressive-looking male you've ever seen?" This was clearly a rhetorical question.

The fair was bigger than ever this year. Everywhere she looked Jolie saw people of all ages in medieval costume. She scanned the crowd for the potential dragon slayer. A tall, bearded Merlin with a hawk on his shoulder strolled past. Jolie turned to Sharon with a questioning look, her voice disinterested when she asked, "Him?"

"Not him," came the disgruntled reply as Sharon jerked her head, indicating the direction Jolie should look. *"Him.* The one with the unicorn."

"Ah, *him."* For once Jolie could understand the attraction. The man was a definite candidate for her friend's "hunk of the month" collection. Sharon dated diligently, apparently looking for some unknown quantity. She had yet to find it, but that didn't seem to dampen her enthusiasm for the search.

Jolie eyed the tall knight speculatively. Much to her dismay, she felt her palms grow damp, her cheeks heat up and a sudden breathlessness overwhelm her. Finally, regaining a bit of her usually formidable self-control, she decided to make light of the moment. "Not bad, Sharon. The unicorn is really cute."

Sharon groaned.

"Mommy, look," Meggie said in the atonal, high-pitched voice characteristic of one who has acquired language primarily through vision. "It a really u-corn. Like my book." The child's face was full of enchantment, and she clapped her hands in excitement.

Jolie knew she was asking a question, even though the inflection was not there. That would come later, along with the other grammatical processes that were necessary for normal speech. For now she was just happy that Meggie was showing an interest in speaking at all.

That she seemed to *want* to talk was no small accomplishment. Not all profoundly deaf children had the desire to speak. The therapist said her progress was a result of Jolie's dedication, of giving Meggie something to talk about and of constantly being someone she could talk to.

Jolie gave Meggie all the credit. Bright and willing, she was quickly becoming a veritable pro at lipreading, advancing beyond even her teacher's expectations. It would all come, eventually, after years of training in breath control, rhythm and stress. Although Meggie's world would always be silent, Jolie vowed that it would never be empty.

"Mommy. See." Meggie jumped up and down on the crate, again clapping in delight. "Look, Mommy. U-corn."

If the handsomely built man did indeed resemble a dragon slayer, the animal he led through the crowd made a passable-looking unicorn.

The milk-white miniature pony was fitted with a little golden horn, and beribboned garlands of flowers were tied around its silky tail and braided into its long, flowing mane. It was an unexpected, charming sight, and squeals of delight followed them. Jolie could easily understand Meggie's fascination, since the child was currently in her fairy-tale phase. She poured over books her "aunt" Sharon had given her, all of them filled with picture stories about elves, gnomes, unicorns and other mythical creatures.

That was the reason Jolie had decided to let Meggie come along today. It would have been unfair to deprive the child of the chance to see knights, princesses and even unicorns in the flesh. But Meggie wasn't used to crowds, and although she seemed to be enjoying herself, Jolie still worried. Despite the demands of running the booth, she'd managed to keep an alert maternal eye on her daughter throughout the morning.

Jolie tapped Meggie lightly on the shoulder to gain her attention. "I think it's a pony in a unicorn costume, sweetie."

"No, Mommy. It real u-corn."

"And he's a real hunk," interposed Sharon.

Jolie laughed at the twin expressions of veneration, hoping her own wasn't quite so easy to read. Score two for the man and one for the animal gamboling at his side.

"Hey, what about Sven? I thought he was the hunk of the hour."

At that Meggie flashed a quicksilver grin, and her eager response was the one Jolie had expected. "Wed."

Jolie nodded. Too bad all their disappointments couldn't be fixed with a red balloon. "You've got it. I'll be back in a few minutes with your blue balloon," she teased.

"No blue." Meggie shook her head vehemently, her smile still firmly affixed. "Wed."

"A red one it is."

Jolie crossed the fairgrounds slowly, passing the many craft stalls offering goods ranging from stained glass to silk-screened garments. Artists were out in full force, and she gave admiring glances to their pottery, oil paintings and woven wall hangings as she passed.

Many other local eating establishments had set up booths, and the heady aroma of exotic foods wafted on the crisp air. She had to sidestep jugglers, mimes and acrobats who wandered around the green, entertaining the crowd.

Little girls in long pastel dresses wore flower garlands in their hair and clutched their parents' hands. Small warriors jousted playfully with wooden swords, and stroller-bound toddlers stared at everything with wide-eyed wonder. The annual event, sponsored by the University of Oklahoma, had grown through the years to a full-scale extravaganza. It attracted hundreds of spectators and participants to the city.

A crowd had formed around an organ-grinder and Jolie stopped to enjoy the antics of his monkey. The tiny creature, dressed in a red and white striped coat and red satin cap, cavorted at the end of his tether. Adults urged children forward to drop coins into the metal cup the little fellow extended. As each coin clinked into the cup, he doffed his hat as a thank-you. The delighted youngsters giggled and demanded more coins. The adults smiled and obliged.

Jolie made a mental note to bring Meggie back later.

Her daughter loved all animals, but monkeys were, to her at least, especially exotic creatures.

Like unicorns. Jolie hadn't seen the unicorn wrangler again and she was annoyed with herself for even looking for him.

Fifteen minutes later, when she returned to the grassy knoll where the food booths were set up, she saw Sharon dutifully waiting on customers lined up around the booth. Good, she thought, business was picking up. It had been her idea to participate in the fair. Although they'd had to hire extra hands to replace them at the tearoom, she felt the exposure they received would help to ensure Quiche and Tell's continued success. In a university town like Norman, restaurants sprouted like mushrooms and were just as permanent.

Succeeding was important to Jolie, and in the eighteen months they'd been in business, she'd invested much of her considerable energy in living up to the reputation they'd quickly acquired. She was determined to make a good life for Meggie, and if she sometimes had to push herself to keep up the pace, she could handle it. Her daughter and her business were her world. She'd found that when she kept her focus that narrow, it wasn't difficult to keep going. That is, as long as she avoided distractions, like Sir Stunning.

Jolie neared the booth, her eyes automatically seeking Meggie's dark head. She couldn't see her but concluded that she was probably playing with her books and dolls on the quilt spread near the back of the booth. Nevertheless Jolie's sharply honed maternal instincts pricked uneasily, and she quickened her pace.

By the time she reached the booth, she was running and out of breath. Fear clutched her heart when she peered into the booth. Meggie's dolls were scattered on the quilt, her books open as though she had been studying the pictures.

But Meggie was gone!

"Sharon!" Jolie grabbed her friend's arm, spinning her around and causing her to drop the change she was making for a customer. "Where's Meggie?"

"She's right—" Sharon broke off in confusion. "Well, she *was* right over there on the quilt looking at her books just a minute ago."

Both of them scanned the crowd, searching for a green-clad elf in the milling sea of bright costumes.

"Oh, Jolie! I don't see her anywhere. Where could she have gone?" Sharon's voice quavered. "God, Jolie, I'm sorry. I thought she was right here."

Jolie knew she should tell Sharon not to worry, that they would find her, that it wasn't her fault the tiny girl was lost among strangers with whom she could not communicate. But all she could think about was her daughter.

Trusting and protected, Meggie had never been alone before. Never. How frightened she would be, unable even to hear her name called, unable to find her way in the tall forest of disinterested adults.

"Look, we have to find her. Don't panic," Jolie instructed Sharon, but was unsuccessful at heeding the advice herself. "You stay here and watch the booth in case she comes back. I'll start looking. She can't have gotten very far."

"Excuse us, miss." A kindly looking older couple near the booth interrupted. "We couldn't help overhearing. We'll help you look."

Several other bystanders voiced their willingness to help search for the lost child.

"Thanks," Jolie said gratefully. "I'm leaving now, but Sharon can describe my little girl for you. She's only four and she's deaf. I'm sure she's very frightened."

She hesitated a moment, not knowing in which direction to look first. She could waste precious seconds on a wild-goose chase. Frantic, she noticed again the open picture book on the patchwork quilt. It was the book Sharon

19

had given her, the one about unicorns. The unicorn! Maybe Meggie had tried to find the man with the unicorn. It wasn't much, but it was a place to start.

Jolie's desperation grew with each passing minute. There were so many people! So many big people. And Meggie was so little. She was much smaller than the average four-year-old. How would she ever find her in such a crowd?

And what if Meggie was looking for her? She had to stop thinking. Searching was her primary concern now. Jolie, still clutching the long string of Meggie's helium-filled balloon, elbowed her way through knots of people without bothering to excuse herself. The balloon bobbed above the crowd, and Jolie prayed the child would see its brilliant beacon and try to reach her.

Every child-snatching story she had ever read or heard on the news knifed through her frantic mind. No, she told herself, Meggie had merely wandered off. No one had taken her. Yet she searched the faces of everyone she encountered in an attempt to discover if any of them was that of a potential kidnapper.

Oh, God, please let me find her soon, Jolie pleaded. She's so trusting, so innocent. She berated herself for never warning her child of potential dangers, but it hadn't seemed possible or even necessary. Meggie didn't have the receptive language ability to understand that there were those in the world who might wish her harm. And besides, she was never out of Jolie's sight unless she was in the protective care of people she trusted.

Meggie would go with anyone who had a friendly face, anyone who didn't frown at her attempts to speak. Limited by her fledgling language skills, Meggie might not even be able to protest.

Please. Please. She means everything to me. She's all I have, Jolie thought desperately.

She stopped at every booth she passed and asked if anyone had seen a little child in an elf suit.

No one had.

Tears were streaming from Jolie's eyes by the time she crossed the bridge over the narrow neck of the duck pond. She hadn't really believed that she wouldn't find Meggie.

Filled with anxiety and helplessness, Jolie decided to return to the booth to see if Meggie had turned up on her own. Maybe one of the volunteer searchers had found her by now. She clung to that thought because it was the only thing between her and hysteria.

She shuddered at what she would have to do if Meggie hadn't been located. She'd have to call the police. Calling in the authorities was like admitting that Meggie was truly lost, that something had happened to her . . .

As Jolie turned back, a flash of green beneath a large leafy elm caught her eye. Her sigh of relief was loud and happy; she'd recognize that tiny form anywhere. She broke into a run.

"Meggie!" she called, knowing that the child couldn't hear the summons. Meggie was absorbed in chasing the bogus unicorn in and out of the dappled shade and couldn't be bothered to risk a glance at anything else. It didn't matter. Just being able to call her name was a joy in itself.

"Meggie!" Jolie grabbed her little daughter and pulled her into a fierce hug.

Meggie tried to squirm away, impatient with her mother for interrupting her new game. "Mommy. You right. She not real u-corn. She dressed up. Tess . . ." Meggie paused thoughtfully, searching her limited vocabulary. "Tess a—ponicorn."

Meggie giggled at her own joke, oblivious to the half-hour of agony Jolie had just experienced. To the child it was merely an adventure, albeit a very big one. "Morgan say she name Tess."

Jolie stared at her uncomprehendingly. Then she became aware of the man who'd sat quietly, propped against the tree trunk, throughout the tearful reunion. He rose agilely, and Jolie found herself face-to-face with the tall Crusader. The plumed helmet was gone, and he no longer looked intimidating at all.

His fine straight nose was perfectly placed between a thick shelf of brows and a neatly trimmed mustache. Jolie noted that both were a shade darker than his sandy blond hair.

His eyes were the deep color of a summer sky, and his lean face was tanned. He smiled, and she watched in fascination as his silky mustache stretched toward the dimple in his left cheek. Jolie tried but found it nearly impossible to remove her gaze from it. He needed the mustache, she noted mentally. It lent a rugged appeal to his otherwise too handsome face.

She felt curiously short of breath and even a bit weak-kneed as she stared at this knight in shining armor. Surely it wasn't this man who made her heart beat a little faster. Jolie preferred to blame her reaction on relief at having finally found Meggie safe and sound.

Despite the romantic traditions of chivalry, Morgan Asher had never fully understood what had motivated the knights of old to do battle over the hand of a fair maiden.

Now he did.

Obviously this petite, flowerlike woman had a child, so she was no maiden. But she fit the damsel-in-distress role so perfectly that Morgan had to smile. Here was a lady for whom he would face the fiercest fire-breathing dragon.

Something intense flared through his entrancement and he recognized the familiar longing for what it was—the heartfelt realization that the shadow-woman who inhabited his imagination actually lived and breathed. He'd finally found the woman of his dreams. He searched her hand for the symbol proclaiming that she belonged to another man.

"I'm sorry you were so worried," he said as Meggie slipped free of her mother's grasp and skipped a short distance away. She tugged the make-believe unicorn along by the silken cord tied around its neck. "We were just about to try to locate you when you found us."

"I was getting desperate," Jolie said unnecessarily.

That was obvious, Morgan thought. When she'd come charging up, she had looked like a cat, with claws bared to protect her kitten. "I asked Meggie where she came from but I didn't catch much of the answer. I think she was giving me a preschooler's version of the facts of life."

He smiled again, and Jolie felt the worry and fear melting away. Then she realized she was staring and had the good grace to be embarrassed. What was the matter with her? She'd thought she was immune to handsome men since Stephen's defection. Jolie was dismayed to discover that she was still vulnerable.

"I'm afraid I've forgotten my manners." The hand she extended was trembling, and she told herself it was from the effects of her ebbing adrenaline. "I'm Jolie O'Day. Thank you so much for finding Meggie for me."

"As much as I'd like to be your hero, I have to confess that she found me." Morgan glanced at the child and the pony, romping nearby. "Or rather she found Tess. It's obvious where her interests lie."

"Well, thank you for taking care of her. I've been worried sick." Jolie realized she was repeating herself inanely, but it wasn't her fault that he had the ability to make her think in circles.

"My pleasure." He held her tiny hand a moment longer than was strictly necessary, reluctant to let her go once physical contact had been established.

Jolie slowly withdrew her hand from his. It tingled from his touch, and she found herself extremely conscious of his virile appeal. She could forgive Sharon for ogling, she realized. If this man got anywhere near her own bed, she wouldn't let him waste time slaying dragons either.

"I can appreciate your concern." He was dying to ask if there was a Mr. O'Day beating the bushes for his lost child. She wore no ring, but that wasn't a totally reliable sign. Yet somehow Morgan sensed that mother and child were alone in the world. Alone and in need of someone's loving care. Maybe that was why there were no laugh lines around Jolie's luminous brown eyes.

He decided to test his theory. "I suppose Meggie's father is looking for her too?"

Jolie glanced up and found the tall knight regarding her intently. He wants to know if I'm married, she thought with surprise, and the tingly feeling was replaced by the old tenseness she always felt in such situations. "Meggie's father and I are no longer together."

It was exactly what he wanted to hear, and Morgan managed to contain his sigh of relief. Sending a warm look in Meggie's direction, he said, "She's a keeper. I can appreciate what it would feel like to lose her."

Jolie didn't think anyone could truly understand a mother's attachment for her only child, but his words were so sincere and his tone so soothing, she nearly believed he could.

Her face softened into a smile, and a slender delicate thread began to form between them. If Morgan had been enchanted by the little girl, it was nothing compared to what he was already feeling for her mother. The O'Days brought out a protective instinct he hadn't realized he possessed. A hot ache formed in his throat.

It was easy to see where the impish Meggie got her looks. He'd been so busy admiring Jolie that he hadn't noticed how alike they were. Jolie's sylphlike beauty boded well for her daughter. Even her period costume seemed as natural as Meggie's elfin one, as if she wore such outfits all the time. He wondered, irrationally, if she had a closet full of wimples and gowns with flowing trains.

"Tell me, Mr.—uh—?"

"Asher. Morgan Asher." Remember that, he added silently. He swept back the hand holding the plumed helmet in a courtly bow. He planned, if it was possible on such short acquaintance, to become significant in her life. His newly ignited emotions clamored when she smiled, and he felt a profound desire to give her many more occasions to do so.

"Mr. Asher, how is it that you were able to communicate so well with Meggie? She usually has trouble with strangers." Jolie lumped him into the category of stranger, although for some reason it didn't seem a fitting description for a man who kindled so many uncomfortably exciting feelings within her.

"Call me Morgan, please. All my students call me Mr. Asher, and it makes me feel so old," he confided with an arresting smile. "But to answer your question, when I heard Meggie speak to Tess I realized that her hearing was impaired. So I made sure she could see my mouth."

He stroked the full mustache that seemed to caress his soft, full lips, and Jolie fought an impulse to push his fingers aside and replace them with her own. "She's a good lipreader for such a young child."

"Meggie isn't just hearing impaired," Jolie clarified. "She is profoundly deaf."

Morgan read the note of defensiveness in her voice, as though the protection of her child had become a battle she now waged instinctively.

"In that case, I'd say her speech is excellent."

Jolie's fighting stance softened at his comment. At least he was a perceptive stranger. "She's progressing nicely. You mentioned your students. Do you teach the deaf?" Jolie could see the interest in his eyes, and his appealing openness disconcerted her. She stepped back to put more distance between them.

"No. I teach medieval history at the university. It figures, doesn't it?" he asked, gesturing first to the pony and then to his own costume.

"Yes, I suppose it does. Somehow I didn't think you were an accountant."

He grinned and, referring to her previous question, explained, "When I was a child, my father lost his hearing in an industrial accident. I guess I just grew up accepting and understanding his deteriorating speech. It's been over ten years since he died, but meeting Meggie made me remember all the old skills. Funny how you never forget certain things."

"Yes, well, thank you again." Suddenly Jolie was eager to get back to the booth and let Sharon know that she had found Meggie. And she was extremely eager to escape Morgan's disquieting presence.

Meggie skipped up to them, her little face puckered with effort as she tugged the reluctant pony along. Morgan kneeled to put himself on her eye level and touched her lightly on the shoulder. "You know, Meggie, Tess is crazy about sugar." He fished into a pocket concealed under his vest of mail. "Take these. She'll follow if you feed them to her." He held out his large palm, and flexed his fingers back, offering the lumps of sugar to Meggie and showing her how to offer them to Tess. She scooped them up, grinning in understanding.

" 'kay, ponicorn. See what for you." The animal perked up at the sight of the familiar treat and suddenly became much more tractable.

Morgan turned to Jolie and grinned disarmingly. "Part of the Crusader's credo: never leave home without it."

Jolie's smile answered his, but she wasn't really listening. She was discovering what it was that had bothered her about this man all along. It was his easy acceptance of her daughter's handicap that made her so cautious. She was thrown off balance by the sudden discovery of something she had despaired of ever finding.

26

She and Meggie had been alone for over three years, and even though she had never sought out men, there had been occasions in the past when she'd accepted dates. None of those men had been able to handle the existence of her deaf child. They were either bewildered by their inability to communicate or jealous of the close mother-child bond. They either pitied Meggie, ignored her or were made uncomfortable by her.

Finally Jolie had decided she could no longer expose her child to their insensitivity and unintentional cruelty. After all, how could casual dates be expected to accept Meggie when her own father could not? So Jolie had stopped going out. She didn't even cultivate many friendships besides those that were necessary to run her business.

She had cast her lot into a lonely ocean of solitude. Now here she was, faced with dry land for the first time. The prospect was both thrilling and frightening.

"Meggie's really getting a kick out of Tess," Morgan said softly as he looked into Jolie's sad, dark eyes. He felt a powerful need to touch her, to pull her into his arms and take her pain away. But that would be foolish and he knew it.

Her expressive eyes had already told him so. He imagined that within their depths he could see heartbreak and joy, determination and desperation, strength and softness, all at the same time. He'd never been so moved by a woman.

"You should bring her out to the house sometime. There's lots more animals there for her to make friends with."

Jolie chose to ignore the open-ended invitation. "She loves all animals. I think it's because there's no communication barrier between them."

"She told me you have a booth here. What are you selling?" Morgan wouldn't have been surprised if she'd

27

answered that she spun straw into gold or spiderwebs into gossamer cloaks.

"My partner and I own the Quiche and Tell tearoom on Campus Corner. We're selling the specialties of the house."

That surprised him. It took strong business sense to run a restaurant in this area. It wasn't that he questioned her skill or her intelligence; it was just that it was difficult to think of her as being rooted in the mundane world of commercial enterprise. She seemed too gentle, too tender for it.

"Good, I'm starved. Why don't I walk back with you?"

It wasn't a question but a statement of his intention. Jolie didn't think she wanted Morgan Asher to walk anywhere with her. The feelings he stirred were best ignored, best forgotten. She'd learned long ago not to trust her instincts about men; they were totally unreliable.

But it was a free country, and he'd said he was hungry. Also, she owed it to Sharon to introduce her to Prince Charming. Besides, once Morgan laid eyes on the vivacious redhead, his heart would be stolen. Men were always attracted to Sharon, so Jolie would be doing all of them a favor.

"Fine with me," she replied with studied nonchalance. "I hope you like quiche and crepes." He looked more like the steak, medium-rare type to her.

"I come from a long line of adventurous epicures. My policy is to try everything at least once," he said with a slow smile.

28

CHAPTER TWO

Meggie was delighted with the organ-grinder's monkey. At Jolie's request, the elderly man let the child place her hands on the hurdy-gurdy to feel the vibrations of the tinny music. Her happy, surprised expression endeared her to Morgan even more. He slipped her a handful of change to drop into the funny little monkey's cup.

As they walked across the green, he observed the attentiveness and patience Jolie exhibited with her daughter. They stopped at a silk screener's booth where Jolie purchased a colorful wind sock, explaining that the child was fascinated by the way the wind moved things. She told him how much trouble she'd had answering Meggie's questions about the sound that wind made.

Morgan had never thought much about wind before, one way or another, but looking at things from Jolie and Meggie's point of view gave him an entirely new perspective.

Being deaf from birth was much harder, he realized, than losing hearing later in life, as his father had. Meggie had no point of reference, no basis for comparison. She was lucky to have so willing a teacher as Jolie.

Shouts of "Mommy look" and "Mommy see" punctuated any conversation the two adults tried to have, and Jolie was grateful for the interruptions. Morgan Asher's seemingly genuine interest only served to unnerve her.

As they passed a giant inflated dragon-shape trampoline filled with bouncing, laughing children, Meggie pulled on Jolie's hand. "Meggie jump. Please."

"Maybe later, sweetie. We have to go back and tell Aunt Sharon that you're safe."

"Aunt Shar worry for Meggie." Only her big brown eyes asked the question.

"That's right. We'll come back later and jump." Morgan Asher had so filled her thoughts that Jolie had momentarily forgotten how frightened she had been earlier. No doubt Sharon and the volunteer search party were still looking.

"Aunt Shar," Meggie yelled as she raced down the knoll, her short legs nearly tangling beneath her.

"Meggie Muffin! Where have you been?" Morgan watched as an attractive red-haired woman scooped the child up just before they collided. Over the tumble of dark curls, she exchanged relieved looks with Jolie, but to Meggie she said, "We were just about ready to call the Missing Muffins Bureau."

"She was on a unicorn quest," Jolie explained before introducing Morgan and telling Sharon how she'd found Meggie.

"Guess I'd better call off the search then, huh?" Sharon asked. "Oh, there's one of the volunteers. I'll have him help spread the word. Excuse me."

"Your partner seems very—nice," Morgan volunteered after Sharon had departed. He'd found her frank appraisal of him rather amusing. He was used to women checking him out. Sharon had given him the same look he got from many of his students and a few of the female faculty members as well.

"Yes," Jolie agreed. "She's more than a partner. She's also a very dear friend." Jolie hadn't missed the look of speculative appreciation and interest in her dear friend's eyes. She'd seen it before often enough. Only it had never bothered Jolie until now. And what bothered her most was the fact that it bothered her at all. Why should she care if Sharon was interested in Morgan Asher?

A moment later a man hefting a minicam on his shoulder approached them. It bore the logo of an Oklahoma City television station. He was accompanied by a young woman with a foam-covered microphone who stepped up to Jolie. "We'd like to film the rest of your story now if you don't mind. Would you mind holding your daughter and looking into the camera?"

"What story?"

Morgan heard Jolie's defensiveness surge to the fore. She drew Meggie behind her as if they were being confronted by a pack of hungry wolves instead of a pleasant-looking reporter and a cameraman.

"What story?" the woman repeated with a reassuring smile. "Why, the Little Girl Lost story, of course. We were lucky enough to pick up on it earlier when the search party was forming. We've been waiting—"

"To exploit a mother's grief if she weren't found?" Jolie supplied.

The reporter winced. "No, of course not. It's just that since she's deaf and since she came back with a unicorn in tow and all . . ."

"I suppose the fact that she's deaf makes the story more sensational." Jolie's voice was cold.

Morgan could tell that Jolie's remarks were rattling the reporter. He intervened. "Jolie, I'm sure no one is trying to exploit Meggie. It's just that the woman probably doesn't get many chances to report happy endings." He smiled what he hoped was his most winning smile. "Am I right?"

The woman's sigh of relief was loud and grateful. "That's right. I'm really only here to cover the fair. You know, getting color and atmosphere? Why, the most sensational thing I've filmed today was the sword swallower." She laughed, but when Jolie didn't join her, she went on. "Your little girl is so cute with her costume and

31

all. And the unicorn makes the perfect touch for a human interest story."

The woman was so earnest that Jolie relaxed a bit. She glanced from Morgan, who nodded encouragingly, to the reporter, who looked appropriately contrite. "Maybe I did jump to conclusions." Jolie didn't feel it necessary to explain her reaction. She'd always been determined not to let anyone draw undue attention to Meggie's deafness.

"So, I can do the story?" the reporter asked with a coaxing smile.

"I suppose so." Jolie picked up Meggie and held her close. The reporter nodded to the minicam operator and cleared her throat. Smiling a bright television smile, she spoke directly into the camera's lens.

"This is Pam Upjohn reporting from the Medieval Fair in Norman. This afternoon a little girl was lost in the biggest crowd ever to turn out for this annual University of Oklahoma event. Concerned bystanders quickly organized a search but it was little Meggie O'Day's mother, Jolie, who found her. It seems she had gone in search of a unicorn . . ."

Jolie didn't listen to the rest of the story. When it became clear that the reporter wasn't going to comment on Meggie's deafness, she looked at Morgan, and he smiled. It wasn't the same kind of intentionally charming smile that he had flashed at the newswoman.

It was a smile of friendship. She wondered why this stranger would want to be her friend. More than that, she wondered why she felt a surge of joy that he did. She'd never had a male friend before and wasn't sure she knew how to handle herself in such a situation.

It had been her experience that most men were not completely honest in their dealings with women, and honesty was a prerequisite for friendship. In her whole life Jolie had never known a man she could fully trust. When the going got tough, the men in her life had opted out. Men were unreliable, at best.

So why did Morgan's warmth and concern touch her as no man had ever touched her before? What did he want from her? And whatever it was, did she have it to give?

The news crew departed, and Morgan turned an appreciative nose toward the booth. "It smells good in there. I think I'll try some of that quiche now. And one of those raspberry tarts for Tess."

Jolie looked at him strangely, then remembered what he'd said about the horse's fetish for sugar. She busied herself preparing the food while Meggie brought Morgan into the booth and seated him on the quilt, showing him the pictures of unicorns in her book.

"See Morgan. Like Tess look," she said earnestly.

"You know, Meggie, I believe you're right. Georgia did a good job getting Tess ready for the fair."

Jolie, who was blatantly eavesdropping, wondered who Georgia was. In fact, she was curious to learn all she could about him. Stop it, she chided herself. Just give the man his food and let him be on his way. She certainly didn't want him hanging around here the rest of the day. Or did she?

Later, after Morgan had finished the quiche and ordered some crepes, Sharon returned with a tall Nordic-looking man in tow. "Well, I managed to call off all the bloodhounds. And look who I found hanging out at the belly dancer's show."

The man grinned sheepishly and nodded to Jolie, then tiptoed dramatically up behind Meggie, who was still absorbed in her book. He lightly clapped a large hand over the child's eyes. She spun around and grabbed his hand.

Jumping up and down, she squeaked, "Fen, Fen!"

"I hear you have big adventure today," he said reprovingly with a mock scowl.

Meggie just smiled, unaware of the alarm she had created, but enjoying all the extra attention. The child boldly informed them she was going to visit Tess, who

33

had not been allowed inside the booth. The ban had caused much disappointment, in child and equine alike. The animal had been tethered to a shade tree nearby.

"Tess lonely," Meggie decided.

Jolie extracted a promise that Meggie wouldn't venture farther. Then she turned back to the adults. "Morgan, this is our friend Sven Larsen. Sven's from Malmö, Sweden. He's here to finish his doctorate in anthropology," she explained.

The two men shook hands. Morgan could tell that the handsome Swede was a lot more to Sharon than just a friend.

"Mommy, look," Meggie demanded.

They all turned to look and found Meggie and Tess both smeared with the remnants of the tarts the child had snitched. From the looks of things, they had worked out an equitable arrangement. First Meggie took a bite and then Tess slurped up what was left of the little pastry.

"Really, Meggie. You shouldn't feed Tess all those tarts." Jolie felt she should at least make the effort to scold her child, but the laughter was trembling in her voice.

"Horses like oats and hay and stuff like that," Sharon spoke up.

Morgan shrugged. "The problem is, Tess doesn't know she's a horse. She's been reared like a poodle. Georgia, my mother, spoils her rotten, and over the years she's developed quite a yen for people food. Twinkies are her favorite things. What can I say? She has weird tastes for a horse."

Tess looked back at them innocently, her large dark eyes moist and doleful. Her dainty pink muzzle, which was now a bright red, nudged Meggie, demanding another treat.

They all laughed, and Morgan said, "As far as Tess is concerned, there are only two speeds when it comes to distributing snacks—too slow and not fast enough."

"Well, I don't know about your lapdog there, but I know a little girl who needs to have some of the afternoon's fun washed off her." Jolie wondered if she had enough Wet-Naps to do the job.

"Why don't you take her on home, Jolie?" Sharon asked. "You look about done in. However, Meggie looks like she could go on for a few more hours."

"How would we get home? And I can't just leave you here alone with the booth. Besides, how would you load everything all by yourself?"

"I'm sure Morgan would be happy to drive you and Meggie home. Wouldn't you, Morgan?" Jolie noticed the matchmaking gleam in her friend's eyes.

"I'd be happy to," Morgan assured them.

Jolie felt as though Sharon had just suggested she sign up for the next shuttle to Saturn. "But the booth . . ."

"I hate to be the one to point this out, Jolie, but we don't have much left to sell. Not counting what the pastry pilferers stole, we had a great day. And Sven can help me load the van. Why let all these gorgeous muscles just sit around and atrophy?"

"I'm ready when you are," Morgan chimed in. This couldn't have worked out better if he'd coached the redhead. He glanced at her and she winked, letting him know that she was aware of his interest in Jolie—and that she approved of it enough to help him out. "It'll take only a few minutes to load Tess into the truck and then we can be off."

"In a truck?" Jolie teased. "You mean she doesn't ride in the backseat of your car?"

"Nope," Morgan replied. "Only when she rides with Georgia."

"Your mother must be one of those permissive parents."

"Yeah, she has a real problem when it comes to dishing out the discipline."

"And I don't suppose she taught you to take no for an

answer, did she?" Jolie sensed manipulation at work but surprised herself by not minding one bit.

"That particular page was missing from her Dr. Spock and she had to skip right over to potty training. I excelled in that." Morgan wanted to see Jolie's elusive smile again and was richly rewarded for his trouble.

Meggie slipped one of her hands into Morgan's, the other into Jolie's. She looked up from one to the other, her dark eyes shining. "Jump first. Then go home."

Jolie knew she shouldn't let anyone as likable as Morgan Asher into her life. Nothing could come of it; but then he wasn't asking for a lifetime commitment. He had only offered her a ride home. Possibly friendship. That she could handle. Maybe.

"C'mon," Meggie pulled them along. "Jump now. Home later."

Jolie looked at Morgan and for a wild moment wondered what it would be like to kiss him, to feel his soft lips and silky mustache on her skin. She could almost feel the excitement his eyes seemed to promise her. He wasn't even touching her, but the child between them acted as a conduit for his warmth. Her instincts were double-timing a clear warning. She decided to ignore them—they had been known to be wrong before.

"What do you say, Mommy? Are you willing to jump?" Morgan's question sounded like a challenge to Jolie.

"Okay," Jolie impetuously accepted. "Jump now. Home later."

As Morgan stripped down to the dark T-shirt beneath the chain mail vest, Jolie wondered what could happen on a moon-walk trampoline? Especially with her daughter and a dozen other people present.

Plenty! Meggie was busy getting used to the bouncy floor of the trampoline and paid scant attention to the grown-ups. Jolie felt nervous and a little silly in the midst of so many frolicking children. Why had she allowed

36

Morgan to talk her into getting into the thing? A silent voice mocked her, and she realized that she'd have a hard time denying any of Morgan's soft-voiced requests. That heart-stopping grin of his totally zapped her resistance.

Cautiously she made her way to an empty corner and sat down to keep an eye on her daughter. She tucked her long skirt around her legs, attempting to retain a little modesty and decorum.

It wasn't long before Morgan followed, but he was jogging, lifting his legs in exaggerated movements, his arms held straight out from his sides. "Get up, Jolie, you old lazybones," he challenged in a persuasive tone. "Come on."

Jolie grinned, shaking her head. "These *old* bones may be lazy, but they're the only ones I have. I'm attached to them and I don't want any of them broken."

Morgan stopped, looming over her, his hands resting lightly on his hips. He flashed a lopsided smile that caused his mustache to reach for his dimple again. His eyes crinkled in the most rake-hell sort of manner. "You must have led a very sheltered life if you don't know how to have fun without getting hurt," he said suggestively, his voice deep and throaty.

"Not exactly," she managed. His intense look did the strangest things to her pulse. It was accelerating at an alarming pace, skipping beats without warning. Her nerves jangled with an inexplicable anticipation. She didn't want to feel like this.

"Well, I think it's time you had a little fun," he said, grabbing Jolie's hands and pulling her to her feet. Even before she could gain her footing, he began moving his weight from one firmly muscled leg to the other, causing her to rock sideways.

"Be careful, Morgan. You're going to make me fall," she warned.

"Lady, those are precisely my intentions," he murmured so low that she had to strain to hear him above the racket of the screaming and screeching children.

She lifted her gaze to his and felt herself being drawn into his heavenly blue eyes. His eyes were too beautiful for a man, his lashes too lavish, she thought dreamily.

It was hot in the mesh tent, crowded as it was with so many warm, active bodies. Morgan was much too close. For now she'd credit the warmth spreading through her to the heat.

She reluctantly tore her gaze from his, only to stare at what she could see of his lips beneath the mustache. He had a gorgeous bottom lip, she mused. It would have to be, to match the beautiful eyes.

"Jump, Jolie," Morgan said enticingly as his hands found her waist. Their glances locked and his eyes held an irresistible combination of humor, caring and desire. Like a bolt out of the blue, Jolie realized that she trusted Morgan.

So Jolie forgot, momentarily at least, that it was unwise to trust men, that she wasn't the type to gaze rapturously into a stranger's eyes or do whatever he wished her to do, and she jumped when Morgan jumped. She also forgot, for an instant, her long skirt, which somehow tripped her bare feet as soon as they were foolish enough to leave the safety of the mat.

That's how they came to fall, one on top of the other, Morgan wrapping her in his arms and Jolie clutching his shirt. Laughing, they rolled over and over and over. When they stopped rolling, their laughter died instantly, and the sounds of frolicking children faded away.

Morgan's eyes maintained their humor, but Jolie could read the intimate promise in them as well. She was tempted as she'd never been tempted before.

"I think you'd better take us home now," she said tremulously, forcing coolness into her tone. It was a difficult task when she felt as warm as melted butter.

"Don't be afraid to have fun, Jolie," Morgan said hus-

38

kily, stroking her jaw with one finger. "It doesn't always have to hurt, you know."

Morgan watched her eyes grow rounder and wider and saw her indecision. He sensed her resolve weakening and longed to hold her, to protect her, to make her his, to give himself to her. The force of this realization shook him, in spite of the fact that he knew it should be too soon to feel such things.

Knowing it would be foolhardy to make a move, but unable to control the wild impulse to kiss her, Morgan gave in to the madness of the moment. With one deft movement his lips swooped down on hers.

His body pressed hers into the air-filled cushion beneath them. One of his legs wedged firmly between hers as their mouths met in a brief but fiercely hot kiss. Jolie surrendered to Morgan's magic, his perfection. His tongue wielded just the right amount of forceful insistence.

Morgan forced himself to keep his hands against the rubber floor. He couldn't risk touching her and losing all track of reality. It was an onerous task, and only the fact that they were in a public place prevented him from losing all semblance of propriety.

Jolie's stomach fluttered, and her heart ached beneath her breasts. At the base of her throat, a pulse beat and swelled as though her heart had risen from its natural place. When his lips left hers they found that pulse, and the touch of his mouth on her bare skin unleashed a whole new torrent of need. This was not the way friendship began.

Jolie pushed against his chest. "Why?" she murmured. "Why did you do that? Why did you have to ruin it?"

Morgan braced himself up and away from her. He wasn't surprised by her reaction. He'd known she needed more time to get used to the idea. He only hoped he hadn't spoiled his chances. He swallowed his passion along with the lump in his throat.

"Sorry," he said, then grinned teasingly. "Maybe I should have practiced a little before kissing you. I knew I was a little rusty, but I never realized I'd make such a bad job of it."

"You know what I mean," she said huffily.

"Maybe you'd better explain it."

"I thought we could be friends," she pointed out sadly. What she didn't point out was that she had trusted him, and look where that had led. He was like all the men in her life, using his charm to get around her defenses, to manipulate her. She was disappointed that Morgan Asher was not different, that he'd shown his true colors so soon.

Then in a firmer tone she added, "I don't want a lover. I don't need one."

"Well," he said resignedly, realizing that he wanted to be much more than her friend, much more than just her lover. He didn't know how he'd become so certain so soon, but he wanted forever. "If it's a friend you want, then it's a friend you've got."

"Sure," she said doubtfully. "Where have I heard that before."

"I'll never let you down, Jolie. You can trust me. From now on I'll be your friend. I'll be the best friend you ever had." His tone was sincere, and all traces of humor and desire were missing from his face as he stared at her intently.

"But you kissed me!" she said vehemently.

"I know," he said huskily. "But I swear I'll never touch you or kiss you again unless it's what you want."

Jolie felt he was telling the truth, and his heartfelt declaration made her stare at him with mixed emotions. She knew instinctively that he was an honest man who would keep to the bargain. That made her happy. However, her own confused feelings about him kept her from answering. She wasn't at all sure she could trust herself in close proximity to Morgan Asher.

"Truce?" Morgan asked.

Before Jolie could reply, Meggie came bounding over to fall across her mother's lap. "Meggie jump. Home now."

She didn't invite him in, but Morgan hadn't really expected her to. They'd chatted about their jobs and the fair and made general small talk, mainly at his instigation. The intimacy of the truck's cab had a quieting effect on Jolie, and she had answered Morgan's questions while refusing to elaborate. Meggie had taken up the slack, bouncing around on the seat, chattering every chance she got in that sweet peculiar little voice of hers.

He walked them to the door, wanting to ask if he could call, afraid she would say no. He didn't have a clue about what to do next, but he knew that he would have to take things slowly with this fragile-hearted woman. He wanted to rid her eyes of that sad, wounded look and he vowed to do it.

He now knew where she lived and he knew where she worked, so it shouldn't be too hard to see her again.

"Thanks for the lift," she was saying. "And thanks again for finding Meggie."

"As I said, she found me. But why quibble over the details, right?"

"Right. Good-bye, Morgan. It was nice meeting you." That sounded banal, and Jolie fully realized it. But she wasn't quite sure of the protocol in such a situation. He had seemed interested enough on that dragon moon walk, but now it didn't look as though he planned to pursue the matter. Perhaps her waspish insistence that he'd somehow done something wrong when he kissed her had discouraged him more than she'd intended.

It had been a long time since a man had made her feel this way. She was filled with ambiguous feelings and needs. And yes, she was forced to admit, desire as well. Part of her wanted to escape back to the solitude of unawakened longings. But part of her thrilled at the memory of Morgan's mouth on hers, at the titillating feel of his weight as they tumbled on the trampoline.

She realized she had created a no-win situation for herself. If he rushed her, forcing his attentions on her, she would be justified in never seeing him again. Yet if he honored her wishes, she would have to suffer the exquisite pain his nearness engendered. If he allowed her to set the pace, was she up to the task? Should she listen to her mind or her heart?

"Good-bye, Jolie." He swept Meggie up into his arms and kissed her cheek, even though it was her mother he longed to embrace. "And good-bye to you, Miss Meggie. From now on you'd better stick to your mommy like"— he grinned—"all that raspberry jam on your face."

Meggie giggled when he kissed her sweet, sticky cheek before passing her to her mother's waiting arms. Morgan wanted to kiss Jolie as well, but this time he restrained the impulse. She'd probably scream for the cops if he tried that again. As it was, she looked ready to bolt, her big eyes filled with some emotion he could not name.

In the past when he'd found a woman who attracted him, he hadn't worried about what to do next. If he'd been too slow making his play, the woman usually took care of the preliminaries.

But Jolie was sending him mixed signals. He was having a hard time decoding them and an even harder time acting on them. He was so worried about doing the right thing that he could do nothing at all. After all, he had promised to let her make the next move.

"Bye," he said again.

"Bye."

Morgan watched them go inside and wondered what it would be like to be included in the warmth of their little home. He hoped someday to find out.

CHAPTER THREE

Jolie fumbled for the telephone on the bedside table. "Hello?"

"Jolie? This is Morgan."

She glanced at the clock: 8:05 in the A.M.? What was he doing calling her so early on a Sunday morning? It had been quite late when she finally went to sleep the night before.

She hadn't been able to get him or that damn kiss out of her head, and she had replayed the afternoon's events over and over. Still confused by her feelings, she had hoped he would call yet was afraid that he would. In the small hours of the night, she'd decided that the best course of action was to forget him. If she could.

"Jolie? Did I wake you?"

"No. I had to get up to answer the telephone." She let the smile on her lips seep into her words.

"I did get you up. Hey, I'm really sorry. But I wanted to call you early before you made other plans for the day." She didn't say anything, so he rushed on. "Have you made other plans for the day?"

"No-o-o," she hedged. "The restaurant is closed on Sundays, and we only signed up for the first day of the fair."

"Great. I'd like you and Meggie to come out to the house today. Meggie can get acquainted with the menagerie, and the two of you can meet my mother." Morgan wanted to ask her out; he longed for the two of them to spend the evening in some dimly lit place. But he didn't want to make it easy for her to refuse. It was too soon for dimly lit places and he knew it.

Meet his mother? Despite her inner protests to the contrary, Jolie wanted to see Morgan again. But she didn't think she was ready to meet his family.

He didn't give her time to demur. "Look, Jolie, I'll level with you. Georgia is giving one of her infamous dinners, and I'd like you and Meggie to come. She writes cookbooks and she makes up a lot of strange concoctions to try out on her guests. I'm afraid she's not above using her family and friends as guinea pigs, but I'm a walking testimonial to the fact that no one has ever died from her dishes."

"That's very encouraging, Morgan. I've always wanted to be awakened from a sound sleep to be invited to partake in culinary research. Thanks for the invitation, but—"

"Don't say no, Jolie. I told Georgia all about you and little Meggie and she really wants to meet you. My aunt and one of Mother's friends will be here, so you won't be alone with me. Although with them, you might wish you were. Please." He had never begged a woman before, but he sensed Jolie's indecision and decided that begging had its merits.

"I don't know, Morgan. Meggie has some weird eating habits, and four-year-olds don't make the most charming dinner companions, you know." Jolie wanted to accept, yet she knew if she did, her life would never be the same.

"No one will notice. Believe me. Georgia invented weird eating habits." Again Morgan yearned to ask her out on a real date, just the two of them in a cozy, romantic atmosphere, but he'd settle for what he could get. Jolie didn't quite trust him, he knew, but she would. He'd see to it. Until then he'd be the soul of gallantry.

"Well . . ." She couldn't think of a better way to

spend the day than to be with Morgan Asher. Just hearing his voice made shivers chase up and down her spine. But meeting his mother?

"All right," he said seriously. "I didn't want to have to resort to this but I can tell heavy artillery is needed here." He paused, crossed his fingers for luck and added what he hoped was the clincher. "Tell Meggie she can ride Tess and that my cat has eight kittens."

"What? If I tell her that it'll make the odds two against one." Jolie turned over in bed and propped herself on her elbows, delighted with the idea that Morgan wanted her company so badly that he would resort to coercion.

"I could come over there and tell her myself. But then I'd feel compelled to tell her I also have a pet raccoon and that the place is lousy with flop-eared bunnies." Jolie wasn't the kind of mother to deprive her daughter of so many furry playmates or his name wasn't Morgan Asher.

"Don't you dare. She'd never forgive me if I let her miss out on eight kittens, not to mention bunnies too." What would be the harm in allowing Meggie such a pleasure-filled day? she wondered. And what was the harm in giving herself a little pleasure as well?

"Then you'll come?" Morgan didn't know what he would do if she refused, because come hell or high water, he planned to see Jolie today!

"Well . . ." She wanted to say yes, but she was worried that the friendship Morgan had offered would blossom into much more. Although she felt she could trust him, she wasn't at all sure about herself. She felt as she had at the age of six when she'd been faced with jumping off the high diving board at the swimming pool. Once she took that fatal leap there would be no turning back.

"Just say yes, Jolie." Morgan closed his eyes, waiting, willing her to accept.

Jolie took a deep breath and, ignoring the warnings of her heart, said the magic word. "Yes."

* * *

"So what time is he picking you up?" Sharon asked as she arranged the skirt of her shell pink sundress on Jolie's overstuffed love seat.

Jolie looked at her watch. "Any minute." Sharon had come over for coffee and refused to leave until she had wormed out every detail of the impending date. That was one disadvantage of renting the other half of your duplex to your best friend: no secrets.

Meggie skipped into the room. She had been so excited when Jolie told her the plans for the day. Having no concept of time, she'd bugged her mother for hours wanting to know how much longer until six o'clock. It was nearly that now.

"Hadn't you better get ready then?" Sharon asked with a puzzled look.

Jolie had taken great pains choosing her outfit. "Okay, I'll bite. What's wrong with the way I look?"

"All you need is a polo pony on that knit shirt and you'd look just like any other aspiring yuppie going for beer and pizza. Don't you think it'll be a shock to Morgan after your Lady Guinevere ensemble?"

Jolie looked disparagingly at the front-buttoned skirt she wore and knew it was true. But she wasn't Lady Guinevere, and Morgan would have to get used to the idea. "I can't help it if I'm conservative."

"You should take a few lessons from Miss Meggie the clothes horse." She turned to the little girl, who was busy tapping her sandals on the wooden floor. "Twirl around again and let me see that skirt spin." She accompanied her words with appropriate hand signals, and Meggie obliged by pirouetting in the middle of the living room floor. Her yellow flowered dress was busy with ribbons, lace and flounces, but on her it looked perfect.

"You look just like a buttercup, sweetie," Jolie told her with a smile.

"So what does that make you?" Sharon asked dryly.

46

There was no flower to compare her drab khaki and navy outfit to. Jolie suddenly felt like a meter maid.

"I'm not at all sure I want to attend this little soiree. I'm especially not sure I want to meet Morgan Asher's mother. I'm not even sure I should see him again."

"Oh yeah, right. Really, Jolie, you are the only woman I know who would have qualms about going to dinner with a warm, intelligent, not to mention sexy-as-hell guy. You obviously do not understand the market or you wouldn't think twice. Sometimes I worry about you."

"I just think it's strange for a man his age to live with his mother. I think it's even stranger that he consorts with a hyperactive unicorn in need of a sugar fix."

"Jolie, he teaches medieval history, for God's sake. Dressing up like a knight in shining armor must be second nature to him. As for the 'unicorn,' he said it was all his mother's idea. And speaking of his mother, maybe she's just here visiting."

"Maybe, but I don't know a thing about Morgan Asher that recommends him as a dinner companion." That wasn't quite true. She knew more about him than she wanted to know. She knew he had the power to steal her good sense when his lips touched hers. She knew the overall effect he had on her. And she knew how Meggie responded to him. She knew him, all right, but her old insecurities were making her wish she'd been strong enough to resist the temptation to see him again.

"So you don't know him. Yet. You knew Stephen all your life and what good did that do you?"

"I loved Stephen," Jolie defended. "At least I thought I did." At Sharon's inquiring look, she added, "You're right."

The redhead brightened. "I am? And you're willing to admit it?"

"Yes. I'm really not a very good judge of character where men are concerned. Even good old Stephen fooled me."

"From what you've told me, Stephen fooled everyone."

Jolie was pensive. "We did love each other. If I don't believe that, then I wasted three years of my life."

Sharon tipped her bright head in Meggie's direction. "Is that so?" She scooted down the couch and hugged Jolie with sisterly affection. "You're twenty-six years old. It's time to start building a future and stop varnishing the past. You can't go on living just for Meggie. What happens when she grows up? When she's gone? How do you think she'll feel knowing her mother sacrificed her life for her?"

"I'm not sacrificing my life. I'm just trying to make sure that she has a good one." Jolie had already considered the things Sharon was warning her about. Many times.

"I know that. You've done a wonderful job with her. No one could have done better. But let her go a little. Let yourself go a little. It's not an act of disloyalty for you to love someone else too."

Was Sharon right? Was she hiding behind Meggie because she was afraid of being hurt again? She smoothed her damp palms down the sides of her skirt. What would she talk to Morgan Asher about? What did he expect of her? Would he be sorry he'd made the first move when he saw the real Jolie O'Day? After all, they wouldn't be in the romantic, rarefied atmosphere of the fair tonight.

Sharon was right. She wasn't dressed properly at all.

She jumped up, intent on finding something more feminine in her closet full of conservative, no-nonsense clothes. "Do you think I have time to change?"

The doorbell chimed and Jolie's heart thudded. Sharon got up to answer it and grinned over her shoulder. "Nope."

Morgan looked even bigger in normal clothes. He was dressed in comfortably faded jeans and a pale blue T-shirt. The sleeves of his expensive, linen-looking sport

48

coat were shoved up to his elbows. His loafers were polished and worn without socks.

Sharon said hello and good-bye as she slipped out, closing the door behind her. Jolie was left facing Morgan, who seemed to loom in her tiny entry. So he wasn't just a figment of her imagination. He wasn't just the fancifully dressed knight who had come to her rescue. Jolie stood, suddenly tongue-tied, trying to think about what she might be able to say to him, but nothing came to mind. She told herself Morgan Asher was just a man.

Just a man? He was a real man. And she was about to go out on the first date she'd been on in a long time. Even if her daughter was acting as chaperon, she was nervous as hell.

"Morgan." Meggie filled the breach charmingly by throwing herself against his long legs. "Where Tess. I can ride Tess. Did you bring kitten to Meggie."

"Slow down. One question at a time. Tess is waiting for you at my house." He scooped her up and held her at arm's length. Winking, he added, "What a lovely riding habit." Setting the child back on her feet, he turned to her mother.

This was a different Jolie indeed, he thought. His glance raked from her smooth don't-touch-me hairstyle down to her utilitarian espadrilles. Was she purposely trying to turn him off? If so, it wasn't working. She merely looked like the businesswoman she claimed to be, not the woman out of a different age that he'd met the day before.

"You look great, Jolie," he said gallantly. When she wrinkled her nose at him in disbelief, he decided to tease her. "But then I've always been a sucker for a gal in uniform."

She looked at him archly, as though she had expected some sort of criticism. "Really? Then I'll wear my old Girl Scout outfit next time."

"That's fine. Just so long as we both know there will be a next time."

Their eyes locked and they exchanged a look that was full of the possibilities blossoming between them. A whisper of wonder rippled through Jolie and she knew she would have to guard her heart carefully. Morgan posed a serious threat to her previously complacent and emotionally deadened existence.

"You look different," she said in an effort to break the tension between them as they headed out to the driveway. "Very *Miami Vice*-y."

Morgan chuckled, and the vibrant sound was like sensual music. Jolie liked the way his eyes crinkled when he smiled and found herself looking forward to his company. She'd had a sample of his wit and zesty humor and a taste of his controlled passion on the moon walk. His admiring look fed her confidence, and she was beginning to think she was ready for more.

His white 1957 Chevrolet convertible was a surprise. Classic in every sense of the word, it was in mint condition and gave Jolie further insight into Morgan's personality.

They all piled into the front seat when Morgan explained that the back would be too windy. Meggie insisted on sitting at the window, so Jolie found herself sandwiched between her squirming daughter and a man whom it would definitely be unwise to sit too close to. He put his arm around her and dragged her left of center, as if she were unable to move under her own steam.

"You're squashing Meggie. Make room for that dress of hers. There's lots of empty seat over this way."

"That's very thoughtful of you," Jolie said, wondering if he planned to drive with only one hand. It might not be safe, but his touch made her feel protected.

"Just one of my many qualities," he said, flashing her a smile before he removed his arm from her shoulder and pulled into the flow of Sunday evening traffic.

50

"Oh," Jolie teased, "you mean you have more than one good quality?"

"Yes, and you'll find out all about them as we get better acquainted." Stopping at a red light, Morgan turned to Jolie and said with a sheepish grin, "I think I'd better warn you that my mother is not exactly Harriet Nelson or June Cleaver."

"She's not Morticia Addams or Granny Clampett, is she?" Jolie joked in a worried little voice.

"No, but she falls somewhere in between. Don't get me wrong. I love her just the way she is. I'm simply trying to prepare you." But how could he prepare anyone for the manic eccentricity of his family? Jolie and her reaction to his family were important to him.

"Prepare me for what?" Georgia Asher was probably a regal, overbearing female who thought all women were after her baby boy, Jolie decided. So the two of them should get along just fine, because she wasn't after anyone. Not that Morgan wouldn't be a prime candidate, if she were in the market.

Just sitting close to him made her pulse race, but she blamed that on apprehension at having dinner with his gourmet mother. Surely it wasn't her libido rearing its timorous little head.

"Just keep an open mind and don't eat anything you don't readily recognize."

Sound advice if she'd ever heard it. "Tell me about your family, Morgan. Do you have any brothers or sisters?"

Morgan laughed delightedly. "No, I'm an only child. I came to my parents in their golden years. I don't think either of them ever quite got over the shock of having a child at that late date. Sometimes Georgia doesn't know what to do with me. I've *never* known what to do with her," he added as an afterthought.

"That explains it." Jolie hadn't meant to voice that conclusion but it was too late now.

"What does it explain?" Morgan prompted.

"Well," she began uncomfortably, "most bachelors your age don't live with their mothers, but it would be logical if she were elderly and needed your care."

Morgan grinned. "Whatever you do, don't ever let Georgia hear you call her elderly. And never mention senior citizens either. She's very active and young for seventy-five. She claims it takes at least ten years to get used to how old you are." Morgan laughed again, then sent her a sideways glance. "How old do you think I am?"

"Well . . ."

"I'll make it easy on you. Thirty-three. And if you're worried about me being tied to my mother's apron strings, let me set your mind at ease. Georgia moved back to Norman a few months ago with plans to live with her older sister. But since they fight like cats in a bag, I invited her to live with me. God knows, I have plenty of room.

"But apparently she shares your view of bachelors living with their mothers, because she turned me down flat. Claimed having her around would cramp my style. Frankly, I think she's more worried about me cramping *her* style."

"So she decided to stay with your aunt?"

"Only temporarily. But that situation really is impossible—you'll understand why when you meet Aunt Nevada. Independent free-thinker that Georgia is, the only way she'd agree to move out to the country was if I agreed to let her have her own place. I'm building a small cottage on the other side of my property for her. It's not ready yet, which is why she borrows my kitchen for her little dinner parties, but she absolutely refuses to live in the same house with her grown son."

Morgan didn't go on to explain that he enjoyed having Georgia around at those times. The house he'd built was big and empty, and he'd never been one to enjoy solitude.

52

He had lots of friends, even loved crowds, but he'd always felt he was missing something because he'd never had anyone special to share his life with. In the past he'd wondered if he'd set his expectations impossibly high, and doubted if he'd ever find what he was looking for.

Until now. If he could find his way into Jolie's heart, he would be set up for his happily ever after.

They left the city limits and traveled east on Highway 9. Morgan turned onto a blacktop road that seemed to stretch endlessly before them. When he'd mentioned that he had a place in the country, Jolie had assumed that he meant the *same* country.

They turned again, this time onto a narrow dirt road thickly surrounded by blackjack trees and dense undergrowth. Early spring wildflowers made bright splashes of color in the blanket of greenery, and the air was full of busy insect sounds.

Jolie enjoyed the rich sweet smell of the earth and loved the riffling fingers of wind in her hair. Morgan didn't seem like the type to want to live so far away from the city lights, but then she acknowledged that she really didn't know him at all.

Morgan glanced at Jolie, her eyes closed behind her amber-color sunglasses. He'd tried to draw her into conversation about herself, but she'd managed to answer all his questions without divulging any real information. He would respect her reticence. For now. But sooner or later Jolie O'Day would have to come clean with him about who, or what, had made her so insecure.

The car stopped and Meggie squealed, "It a castle. A really castle."

Jolie opened her eyes and saw that they had braked on a curving gravel driveway in front of the most beautiful house she had ever seen. Meggie wasn't far wrong in her pronouncement.

The large house was built of light gray stone and sported two turrets and a moat. A moat? Jolie blinked to confirm her first impression. It was a moat, and it had a drawbridge.

"Mommy look." Meggie was bouncing again, this time on Jolie's lap. Any chances of making it into the house wrinkle-free were shot. She took her daughter's advice and looked closer. She saw that the moat was really a stream and that a footbridge had been cleverly constructed to resemble a drawbridge. She hoped the turrets were real, for she could already envision winding stone steps leading up to the tower rooms.

This was simply too much! A knight in shining armor with a unicorn yesterday, and a veritable castle today. This man was not to be believed.

Morgan hopped out of the car and took Jolie's hand in a courtly manner. "Welcome to Quantum Leap. My humble home."

"It would only be humble if you allowed the architect to build those turrets for decoration." Jolie's breath caught in her throat when Morgan bowed his head, touching his warm lips to her trembling hand. His gesture ignited a little spark of electricity that zipped right up her arm. She wasn't falling for any of this, was she? Of course not.

It was all this knight-in-shining-armor business. Wasn't it every woman's dream to be carried off to a castle by a handsome knight? Nonsense. Maybe that was every little girl's dream, but Jolie reminded herself she wasn't a little girl anymore. Yet when Morgan's eyes bored into hers, bees and butterflies seemed to churn in her stomach.

He let her step aside and reached in for Meggie, who was about ready to climb over the seat and out the back. "Not so fast, young lady. If you ruin that dress, your mommy might throw both of us in the dungeon."

Meggie's eyes widened. "A really dungeon."

"No. I was just kidding. All I have is a basement in which the only means of torture are jars of Aunt Nevada's pickled okra."

Meggie looked confused but skipped a short distance away, intent on exploring the fanciful drawbridge.

"Why do you call the house Quantum Leap, Morgan? I'm afraid the connection escapes me." Jolie was more than a little intrigued by this compelling man and his unusual home.

"A quantum leap is any sudden and extensive change or advance. When I started building this place, it was certainly a change from the trailer I'd been living in. Also, since I'm teaching medieval history, I became fascinated by the castles of Europe. I thought it would be fun to build an Okie interpretation."

They stood on the little bridge listening to the slow-moving streamlet wash over moss-covered stones. Jolie raised her brows in question. "You built this place? You personally? With your own two hands?"

Morgan grinned, and she detected the pride in his voice. "Stone by stone. But don't look so impressed—it took me over five years."

Jolie was impressed, more than ever. She was about to ask more when Meggie interrupted. "Mirrors why," she asked, obviously referring to the art deco mirrors placed at random in the flower beds.

"Those are for Valentino."

As if he'd been summoned, a beautiful peacock strutted self-importantly around the corner of the house. Taking one look at his captive audience, he splayed his bright feathers to be admired.

"Valentino is so vain. He used to crash into the window seeking his reflection until I thought of the mirrors." Morgan ushered Meggie and Jolie toward the front door. "Let's get inside before the harem arrives. They're never far behind him."

"Bootiful bird," Meggie cooed.

"What are the peahens' names?" Jolie couldn't resist asking.

"Scarlett, Amber and Darlene."

55

Jolie laughed. "I can place Scarlett and Amber in their proper literary reference, but tell me, what romance produced Darlene?"

Morgan ducked his head sheepishly. "One I had in first grade." He flashed his infectious grin and added, "So call me sentimental."

CHAPTER FOUR

Morgan held the door and Jolie and Meggie stepped inside. The walls of the large foyer had been created of the same gray stone as the exterior. They soared up to the second story, and a brilliantly lit brass chandelier sparkled high over their heads. A wide expanse of lushly carpeted stairs curved upward, and Jolie could see the open balcony of the second floor landing.

If this was where a professor could afford to live, the state regents were mishandling taxpayer funds.

Jolie commented on this to Morgan.

He laughed. "I'm sure it may look that way to you, but rest assured that I built this place on money I inherited." He paused. "Let's go into the dining room. There'll be time for a tour later if you're interested. And a special tour outside for you, Meggie me darlin'."

Morgan led them through the foyer and what was probably the living room, although to Jolie the term didn't do the room justice. It was a hodgepodge of design, antiques and contemporary pieces vying for attention. There was silver gray carpeting underfoot and massive wooden beams overhead. The fireplace looked wide enough for Jolie to stretch out in, and she wondered if it was for the roasting of whole oxen.

The art pieces were as eclectic as the furnishings, and she recognized some of the signed lithographs. She twirled, trying to take it all in, and decided the room was as marvelously unpredictable as its owner.

The dining room could have been the set for a remake of *The Saracen Blade*. The walls were covered with a pewter-colored paper, and two huge tapestries faced each other on opposite walls. Jolie noticed with amusement that one of them was a reproduction of the famous unicorn tapestry.

The table was long, heavy and ancient-looking, with ten high-backed and rush-seated chairs surrounding it. An imposing chandelier of aged pewter swung above the finely appointed place settings.

Three people stood around a hunt table on the far wall, talking and sipping tiny glasses of liqueur.

Morgan handled the introductions the way he did everything, with panache. Georgia Asher was not the tall, regal snob Jolie had anticipated. She was a tiny sprite with a headful of frizzy, henna-red curls. She wore bright red and black flowered hostess pajamas that flowed as if with a mind of their own and hindered her movements. They were obviously causing her a great deal of aggravation.

A stack of thin silver bracelets on both arms jangled when she gesticulated, which she did often. Surprisingly, the woman was warm and glittery. Jolie quickly decided that Georgia Asher had a gritty kind of grace.

Meggie and Georgia hit it off immediately, and Jolie knew Morgan had briefed her about the child's special needs. But then she remembered Morgan telling her that his father had been deaf and realized that that probably accounted for the woman's ability to communicate with Meggie. Before long one stack of bracelets had been transferred from Georgia's scrawny arm to Meggie's tiny one.

The older woman held a sheaf of papers in her hand. "Morgan, I can't make out the timing on this recipe. I've misplaced my damn glasses again."

Morgan kissed the lined cheek. "Watch your language, dear, we have guests." He gently pulled the lost spectacles from the mop of curls and positioned them on the bridge of her nose.

"I'm not senile yet, dammit. I know we have guests." Her skinny elbow struck Morgan's hip.

"You'll have to excuse Mother—she curses like a sailor. You see," he explained in a confidential tone, "she loves to shock people."

Georgia laughed gustily. "Now I remember why I had you so late in life, and why you are an only child." She turned to Jolie. "You'll find, my dear, that children can be a lot like Social Security—they never turn out to be quite the comfort in your old age that you expected."

"Now, love, you know I've always had the greatest admiration for you, and I happen to know that you adore me." He grinned down at his slight mother and tweaked her cheek. "Father loved to tell me how you nagged him until you finally became pregnant."

"Bull—" Georgia stopped mid-oath when her son held up a restraining hand. "He didn't tell you any such thing," she scoffed. "Your dear father was too refined to talk like that. Besides, your education has been shamefully neglected if you think nagging will do it." She shook her head in mock sadness. "I've taught you everything you know, so I have no one to blame but myself."

It was easy to see that Morgan and Georgia had a very special relationship. Anyone would admire the teasing closeness they shared. With a start Jolie realized she was beginning to admire too many things about Morgan Asher.

When Morgan introduced his aunt Nevada, he explained that she and Georgia were named for the states of their birth. As Georgia pointed out, it could have been worse; their dear departed brother had endured life with the ungainly name of Alabama.

Aunt Nevada was the antithesis of Georgia. She was

59

quite large, and her blue-rinsed hair was pulled to the back of her head in a constrained bun. She wore a shapeless black skirt, a no-frills white blouse and orthopedic shoes. She was argumentative, with a trace of friendly hostility.

Jolie couldn't decide if Nevada was hard of hearing or just hard-headed, but everything had to be repeated for her at least twice. Her slavering white bulldog, Roderick, evidently suffered the same affliction, for when told to leave Jolie and Meggie alone, he waited until he'd drooled all over their feet before obeying.

Aunt Nevada was not too concerned with Roderick's lack of manners. She was much too busy grilling Morgan as to the whereabouts of a woman named Monica Jenet. Evidently she was accustomed to finding Monica in Morgan's company, and Jolie couldn't help wondering what role the woman played in his life.

Then she chided herself for caring so much. It was natural for Morgan to have women in his life; she'd worry if he didn't.

"I think she went to Tulsa," Morgan said vaguely. Why did Aunt Nevada have to bring up Monica today? Either it was an unlucky conversational gambit or sheer perversity on her part.

"Where?" Aunt Nevada snapped.

"Out of town," Morgan retorted, his voice a little too loud to be polite. Subtlety just didn't work with his aunt. "Out of town," he repeated for good measure.

Barnaby Dibble was a delicate, ascetic-looking man. Jolie was a little surprised to learn that he, like Georgia, was a writer and that his work had been published in detective and confession magazines. She was not at all surprised to learn that he "kept company" with the widow Asher.

They sat down to dinner at the table, beautifully set with twinkling crystal and sparkling silver and adorned by a candelabra and fresh flowers. Morgan's mother pre-

60

sided at the head of the table, with Barnaby and Nevada seated to her right. Meggie, Jolie and Morgan were seated opposite them.

Georgia rose, clanging her spoon on a glass and yanking her sleeve out of her water goblet. "My chapter this week is called 'Getting into Chicken.' Please feel free to critique honestly." She took her seat, frowned and dabbed at her dripping sleeve with a yellow linen napkin.

Morgan groaned. She always said that, but no one ever took her up on the offer. He leaned toward Jolie and whispered behind his hand, "Oh, damn, it's worse than I thought."

"What?"

"Her chapter. Georgia is a literal person, so I'm sure she means getting *into* chicken. There are some revolting things inside chickens, so don't eat anything that looks suspicious. When I take you home we'll grab a hamburger."

"Shhh," Jolie warned. "You'll hurt her feelings."

"Hamburger?" Nevada asked querulously. "Did you say hamburger, Morgan?"

Barnaby peered around a bouquet of spring daisies and adjusted his bifocals. "I believe," he said with a wink at Morgan, "our Morgan was telling us that this was better than hamburgers, Nevada." Then he turned a loving gaze on Georgia. "That's quite a compliment coming from our Morgan, isn't it, dear? We all know how much he loves hamburgers."

Morgan smiled benignly, but Jolie could have sworn she heard him moan.

She and Meggie were introduced to Leah and Daniel, who served the mysterious dishes. The young couple was working their way through college by doing odd jobs around the Asher place. They lived in the trailer Morgan had vacated and chatted amiably as they placed dish after dish of disguised chicken on the table. There were no vegetables, no salad, no condiments, not even a crust of bread. Just chicken incognito.

Jolie was wondering how she would go about making the best of such a situation when suddenly Morgan's naked foot caressed her leg. She sucked in a deep breath, refusing to look at him.

"Stop that," she hissed.

"What?" Nevada bellowed. "What did Morgan do?" Every eye turned to Jolie, waiting for her answer.

"Uh—Roderick," she exclaimed, thinking quickly. "He keeps licking my foot."

Morgan winked fiendishly before he resumed his temporarily interrupted game of footsie.

Nevada glanced at the fat dog, who lay in a placid heap under the table, then eyed Jolie doubtfully throughout the remainder of the meal.

Jolie shot Morgan her best drop-dead look, but those toes of his were doing naughty, suggestive things to her leg and her libido. She knew the rush of heat she felt had stained her cheeks pink and she found herself extremely conscious of Morgan's virile appeal. So conscious, in fact, that she sincerely doubted her ability to eat another bite of food.

She tried to ignore the pulsing knot that had formed in her stomach and focus her attention on Meggie. It wouldn't be in her best interests to dwell on the sensual game Morgan was playing under the table. It also wouldn't be a good idea to call undue attention to it.

Meggie was happily munching the peanut-butter-and-banana sandwich she had requested and received on a pretty flower-sprigged Spode plate. She was totally unhelpful when it came to distraction.

Morgan was thoroughly enjoying himself. It did his male ego good to see the pretty blush on Jolie's cheeks and the sparkle of panic in her eyes. He noticed her squirming nervously. If his foot alone could inspire such quivering havoc, it boggled his senses to think what the rest of his body could do. He winked at her and went for an instant replay.

When Morgan's foot slid sinuously up her calf, caressing her skin through the filmy barrier of her stockings, Jolie considered under what pretexts she could leave the table. Short of shouting "Fire!" none came to mind.

"What do you call this succulent dish, my dear?" Barnaby gushed.

Georgia preened under his flattery. "That one is called Beggar's Delight."

Morgan whispered for Jolie's ears only, "Also known as fricassee of beaks and claws."

Jolie grinned and sent Morgan another killing look, aimed at making him cease and desist his intimate acquaintance with her legs. He winked and allowed his own long leg to rest dangerously near hers under the cover of the table.

Barely suppressing the laughter she felt at the innocent look on his face, Jolie decided that the evening was turning out to be entertaining after all.

Barnaby took another bite and gently dabbed at the corners of his mouth with his napkin. "This tastes divine, dear. What do you call it?"

Georgia gestured to a clay casserole dish. "This is one of my favorites: *Cicen Guiser en Sallere.*"

Jolie, hungry, looked hopefully at Morgan, who vehemently shook his head and mumbled, "I think that's French for chicken gizzards in gravy."

Jolie cast covetous glances at Meggie's simple sandwich. She made a vow never again to eat anything from the inside of any animal.

Barnaby patted Georgia's hand fondly. "You're a fantastic chef, my dear."

Georgia blushed becomingly, which looked strangely girlish on her aged features. "Why thank you, Barnaby."

Jolie turned to Morgan, who rolled his eyes heavenward. "What?" she asked.

63

"Poor Barnaby. He's so besotted by Mother he would eat pine bark and praise it to high heaven."

"I think he's cute," Jolie decided.

"Who's cute?" Nevada asked innocently. Apparently her hearing problems were confined to things she didn't wish to hear.

This time Morgan rescued her. "Jolie thinks Valentino is cute but I've been trying to explain what a pain a peacock can be sometimes."

Jolie thought Morgan was cute. She congratulated him silently on his fast thinking, not to mention his podiatric dexterity.

"Ah, Valentino," Georgia trilled. "His beauty far outweighs the nuisance factor, Morgan."

"Hm," he replied vaguely while attempting to remove Jolie's shoe with his toes.

Conversation around the table resumed and Morgan passed a laden platter to Jolie. "Eat that at your own risk," he whispered.

Startled by Morgan's dinnertime hijinks, Jolie yanked her leg up so suddenly that her knee banged the table, rattling the dishes and attracting unwanted attention. Ignoring the curious glances, she scraped a minute portion of the brown crusty things onto her empty plate as though nothing had happened. Remembering a trick from her childhood, she spread them around so it would look as though she were eating.

She quickly passed the unidentifiable fried objects to Morgan, who passed them straight on to Nevada. These were no ordinary poultry dishes; they all seemed to come from inside the bird. Morgan's dire prediction had come true.

Jolie watched uneasily as Nevada raked a generous serving onto her own plate. "What happens if she's working on a chapter of desserts?" she asked when the others weren't listening.

"Then we all get off on a sugar high." Morgan gestured at the dishes on the table. "These are actually in the chapter. You should taste some of the unholy stuff that never makes it to the book." He clutched his throat, stuck out his tongue and crossed his eyes, all before anyone noticed.

Jolie giggled at his antics. "Does she cook like this all the time? Every day?"

"Thank God, no. I only allow her to use my kitchen for her dinner parties. I take care of the daily cooking in this house, and Aunt Nevada guards her kitchen zealously." At her doubtful look, he added, "I learned to cook at an early age. I had to. Self-preservation. Georgia celebrates the completion of each chapter with a one-dimensional orgy, but fortunately she only manages to write about one book a year."

"Morgan," Nevada interrupted. "What did you say Monica was doing in Tulsa?"

"I didn't say, Aunt Nevada." Morgan's voice was level but noncommittal. Act casual, he told himself, and maybe Jolie won't notice that my aunt keeps bringing up the name of another woman. "I believe she went to visit some friends."

"What?" Nevada squinted as if to see better would improve her hearing as well.

"Visiting!" Morgan boomed. "Monica went to Tulsa to visit friends."

"No need to shout, sonny," Nevada said with a sniff. "I happen to like Monica. She's got an adorable accent and last week after dinner she told me she would probably be seeing me in a few days and—"

"Nevada, dear, you're not eating," Georgia intervened. "Morgan, pass the Rice Surprise to your aunt. Nevada loves rice, don't you, dear?"

Morgan grinned sweetly and passed the casserole to his aunt, who accepted the bowl with a frown, muttering, "It's the surprise that I'm worried about."

Jolie wondered why she felt another faint stirring of

jealousy at the thought of Morgan and Monica, whoever she was, having dinner together. And here she was feeling curiously honored to have been invited to meet the man's family. Evidently he took all his women home. All his women? Why, she hadn't even known that he existed last week, so she had no right to feel the way she did. Unfortunately, there wasn't much justice where feelings were concerned.

She also didn't know a thing about the woman with the adorable accent so she shouldn't care if she and Morgan had something going.

Nevertheless, she didn't like thinking of them as a couple. Morgan and Monica. It sounded like an animal handler and his trained seal. The usually generous Jolie was appalled at her own lack of tolerance.

Morgan picked up the rice dish and gave himself and Jolie a hearty dollop, being careful to leave the dark, unrecognizable objects in the bowl.

"Here, this looks harmless enough and it will keep us from starving until we get back to town. It will also make Georgia think we're eating. *Bon appetit.*" Morgan really appreciated how well Jolie was taking everything. Considering the rapacious nature of his feet, he'd have to add grace under pressure to the growing list of things he liked about her.

Jolie grinned conspiratorially. "Thanks."

Tess poked her head through the window, apparently on the mooch, and nuzzled Georgia's shoulder. Mrs. Asher cooed at her and fed her morsels from her plate. No one else seemed to think it odd to have a horse joining them for dinner, and Jolie had to admit that after today's turn of events, even she wasn't too surprised.

"Poor Tess. No more ponicorn," Meggie commiserated.

Everyone laughed when Morgan explained her nickname for Tess. As far as the little girl was concerned, dinner was over now that the entertainment had arrived.

She slipped from her chair and ran to the window and threw her arms around the pony's neck. "Still mine ponicorn."

"I told you Georgia spoiled her." Morgan winked, and his toes fondled Jolie's leg again. He leaned toward her, and his voice was low and inviting. "You look as if you could use a little spoiling. I'd like to be the one to do it."

A tingly warmth spread through Jolie and she wished she could tell when Morgan was teasing. She looked away from his mesmerizing gaze and noticed Nevada's nearly empty plate. As a diversionary tactic, she picked up a bowl and hurriedly offered it to her.

The woman's plump arm shot out in alarm. "No! No more for me. Georgia's really outdone herself with this meal."

"Why, thank you, Nevada," Georgia responded graciously.

Nevada dropped her gaze to her lap, and Jolie watched as Roderick noisily gobbled another bite from the woman's napkin. He hiccuped once and settled into his former position.

Morgan's aunt left right after dinner, claiming she and Roderick needed to go home and rest. Jolie wondered if the dog would receive any of the antacid his mistress was sure to take.

Barnaby and Georgia volunteered to take Meggie outside to see the rest of the animals and to ride Tess. Daniel and Leah began clearing the table, and Jolie found herself alone in the hallway with Morgan.

"We've got to start meeting like this," he said softly just before he took her into his arms.

CHAPTER FIVE

"I'm not going to kiss you," Morgan whispered into the silence that enveloped them.

Damn! Jolie sighed her frustration. Now was a fine time for the Footsie King to turn honorable on her. He'd primed the pump all during dinner and now he didn't want any water.

At her blank look of disbelief, he continued, "Remember my promise? I told you I wouldn't do anything you didn't want."

Jolie remembered all right. It was a promise she'd rashly extracted and was already regretting. However, if he took it upon himself to give in to the spontaneity of the moment. . . .

She had expected, even anticipated, the lush warmth of his mouth on hers. When it didn't come, Jolie bit back her frustration.

Morgan watched as she grappled with her conflicting emotions. Was it his own wishful thinking, or had disappointment cast its shadow across her delicate features?

Ever one to seize the moment, Morgan returned the ball to her court. "Would a friendly hug be out of order?"

She considered. Friendly hugs often led to much more. If one was lucky. "That sounds harmless enough," she said reasonably, trembling for his touch.

Morgan drew her closer. More to remind himself than

to reassure her, he said, "Now, this harmless little hug is just a gesture of friendship. I'm *not* going to kiss you."

Morgan held her loosely in what could not technically be called a clinch. Since he strove for fraternalism and comfort, it would not qualify as a full-fledged embrace. He hadn't known he possessed so much control, but in this case he was glad to have the reserves to tap.

He desperately wanted to taste her pouty mouth again. He wanted to muss her sleek hair and discover all the secrets of her body. He wanted to make her forget about everything in the world except him and the possibilities the night promised.

Instead he forced himself to stop thinking about her small, womanly figure and the unsettling effect it had on him. Trying to ignore the sting of desire that heated his body, Morgan reminded himself of his plans to give her time to make up her mind to trust him.

When she came to him, he wanted it to be her idea. And he would abide by his misconceived plan if it killed him. Discomfort, to his knowledge, had never killed any-one.

I'm not going to kiss her, I'm not going to kiss her. He hoped the litany would serve as sufficient distraction for his growing urgency. I'm not going to kiss her. "I'm not going to kiss her." Caught up in the tantalizing nearness of her, he unintentionally gave voice to his incantation.

Jolie's hands were pressed against Morgan's chest and she felt the erratic heartquake rumbling beneath her palms. He gently massaged her back and his warm breath whispered against her cheek. Her own heart thumped erratically and her blood surged from her fingertips to her toes.

The sweetly intoxicating musk of his body muddled her senses and Jolie was astonished by the delight such a simple touch provoked. The sparks he'd kindled during dinner combusted in a sudden flare of urgent intensity.

She scarcely recognized her own voice when it demanded, "Oh, just shut up and kiss me!"

Morgan had never been a man who needed to be told twice.

When it came, the melding of their lips and the eager communication of their bodies created a transfusion of emotion unlike any Jolie had ever known. She was transported.

Morgan savored the sweet taste of her lips and the tantalizing feel of her supple body pressed to his. A kiss, he reminded himself. All she'd invited was a kiss. There'd been no discussion of ravishment in the foyer.

Setting her gently away from him, he murmured huskily, "Are you ready for that tour now?"

"Tour?" she asked blankly, her pulse still racing.

"Of the house?" He relished her inability to return to earth. Amazing what a harmless little hug could lead to!

"Oh, *that* tour. Certainly." He let her go and Jolie was surprised that she could stand on her own. The expression "weak in the knees" took on new meaning.

They climbed the broad stairs. It was no small feat for Jolie to force her attention from Morgan to the polished elegance of the teak banister. Three bedrooms opened off the upstairs hall. One was decorated in a lavish art deco style complete with satin chaise longue and walnut furniture. Another was ornately Oriental, and Morgan explained the divergent styles; he'd done the rooms at different times and was influenced by his interests of the moment.

He told her the stories behind some of his finds. The brass and porcelain bathroom fixtures purportedly came from a house of ill repute that had been torn down to make way for a less licentious enterprise. Jolie believed the story: the great claw-foot tub looked totally decadent. It was probably designed for tandem bathing. An unchaste image of the two of them so engaged slipped past her vigilant defenses.

70

Morgan's bedroom opened into one of the tower rooms, where an expensive-looking telescope was positioned at one of the tall windows.

"I thought your interests lay in the past," Jolie commented while openly admiring the telescope.

"My interests lie in whatever interests me," he answered with a slow smile. "History is fascinating; it provides a link with the known. Through it you get a sense of belonging."

"And astronomy?"

"Astronomy often deals with the unknown. It creates a sense of wonder." He stepped forward and made some adjustments on the equipment. "Take a look," he invited, "and tell me what you see."

"Stars?"

"I hope so. Do you see that bright one on the left?"

"Yes." Jolie peered through the telescope and felt a bit of the wonder he'd described. He really was full of surprises. "Is it Venus?"

"That's right." Morgan patted the instrument. "It's not Mt. Palomar but it's fine for a hobbyist like me. Tell me, Jolie, what do you do for fun?"

"Fun?" She laughed self-consciously. The pursuit of fun was not part of her daily schedule. In fact, she'd had more fun since meeting Morgan than she'd had for a long time. "What's that?"

"It's worse than I thought." Morgan clucked in dismay. "I can see I have my work cut out for me." More than anything he wanted Jolie to have a good time, to laugh and forget whatever it was that had made her so serious. It didn't seem fair that such a young woman should have to take on so many responsibilities alone. He wondered again about Meggie's father.

Tenderness surged through him and he had to lead the way out of his bedroom. He was suddenly filled with the startling realization that when he'd designed and furnished the room, it had been with someone like Jolie in

71

mind. A sudden tremor of desire made him propel her toward the door before he lost his resolve to remain a gentleman. Chivalry was a pain in the neck. No wonder most people considered it dead.

Jolie tried not to let her glance linger too long on Morgan's bed. But it was difficult to overlook. Dominating the center of the room, it looked more like a separate chamber. She knew little about antiques but guessed the wood-paneled bed to be at least two hundred years old.

Or was it a fabulous reproduction? Heavy draperies were tied back to reveal a mountainous mattress heaped with pillows and fur throws. It was a bed tailor-made for a castle and no doubt the stage for more than a few bacchanalian affairs, a bed straight out of a fantasy.

Her imagination was working overtime. A flashing image of being tossed naked into the sensual luxury of the furs leapt unbidden into Jolie's mind. Before she could banish the vision from her thoughts, she pictured Morgan's bare, muscular body limned golden by the flames from the now cold fireplace.

He was easing down beside her, touching her, giving her ultimate pleasure . . . damn!

Jolie was astonished by the powerful images she had conjured. What was the matter with her? She'd never had such lusty thoughts before. Not only was the atmosphere working on her senses, but the vivid memory of Morgan's sensuous kiss was getting to her as well.

On the way downstairs Jolie considered what she had learned about Morgan so far. A historian who was handy enough to build this amazing house and still have time left for stargazing was undoubtedly unique. She knew he was warm and funny as well as kind and sensitive. That he was also a passionate man who enjoyed sensual pleasures was obvious.

No woman could ever be bored with him—there would always be something new to discover. She tingled with anticipation and excitement even as she acknowledged sadly that Morgan Asher would be too much for her to handle. No matter what her libido clamored for, she didn't need the countless distractions and complications he would bring to her life.

Instead of dwelling on the way he made her feel, she would do well to remember her priorities. Her reservations. Her fears.

"Do you think she overdosed on bunny-snuggling and kitten-cuddling?" Morgan asked with a grin as he and Jolie tucked Meggie between the Snoopy sheets. The little girl had fallen asleep on the drive home and had not stirred while Jolie got her ready for bed.

"Nope. She's just recharging her batteries. She'll be wide awake and raring to go in the morning."

They tiptoed out of her room. "Thanks for showing us both such a good time, Morgan. I enjoyed it as much as Meggie." Too much, she thought.

"I don't see how," he teased, his eyes twinkling mischievously. "You didn't even get to smooch a bunny."

"No problem. Bunnies are pretty far down on my list of things to smooch." But you, she thought, could easily become number one.

"Where am I on your list?" he queried as if reading her thoughts.

Was he teasing again? Jolie wondered where she ranked on his list. What had that stolen kiss meant to Morgan? How she hated playing the game when she didn't understand the rules. She didn't even know whose side she was on.

In a much more flippant voice than she'd thought possible, she quipped, "At least in the top one hundred."

He pretended to consider that and then shrugged good-naturedly. "I guess I can live with that. For now." He picked up the white bag of hamburgers they'd purchased at a fast-food place on the way home. "Let's eat

73

these outside," he suggested, taking her hand and leading her through the sliding glass door to the small deck.

The little backyard was awash with moonlight, and gentle night sounds surrounded them as they ate at the umbrella table. Jolie looked up and caught Morgan watching her in that intense way of his. She could feel his vitality crackling across the table, as though he was willing her to do something, to say something meaningful.

"I think junk food is vastly underrated," she remarked as she bit into her burger.

"Oh, you're just saying that because of the *Cicen Guisier en Sallere.*" Morgan dunked a fry in ketchup and popped it into his mouth.

They laughed and then a comfortable silence settled between them while they ate. Morgan gathered the remains of their feast and stuffed the debris back into the bag.

"I couldn't help noticing the swing. I'll race you to it and the loser has to push!"

"You're on." Jolie leapt to her feet but Morgan's long legs decided the outcome. He was sitting smugly on the swing when she got there.

She stood behind him, filled with uncertainty. She knew what was expected of her—she'd pushed Meggie enough to have that firmly in mind. She just couldn't decide where to put her hands. At her height, his well-formed backside was the most convenient spot. If she stretched she could brace her palms against his muscled back. That seemed the best plan of action. She pushed and ran forward.

She hadn't wanted to touch him at all, knowing that she would once again experience the electrical jolt it caused. But once she made contact with his body it was difficult to let go. So difficult, in fact, that she was nearly struck by the swing as it made the return trip.

Morgan slipped off the swing and gestured to the spot he'd just vacated. "I can see you don't know the first thing about swinging. Poor Meggie." His tone suggested that Jolie's education had been sadly lacking. "Climb up. I'll teach you everything you need to know. I'm a great swinger."

"You've probably had more practice," Jolie wise-cracked as he boosted her onto the seat.

He put a hand on each of her hips. His touch was shockingly sensual, and Jolie wondered again why he had such a profound effect on her. His voice was deep and his words provocative as his thumbs massaged her hipbones lightly. "We move forward." He matched action to words in slow motion and tightened his grip. "We move back."

"Uh, Morgan . . ." Jolie didn't mean for her voice to be a breathless whisper but how could she help it? He was very distracting.

"Shhh," he whispered near her ear, his thumping heart against her back, causing Jolie's stomach to constrict. "I'm giving lessons here." And it would pay to keep his mind on that, he thought wryly. She felt so soft to his touch, so warm. It would be easy to blow his plan, to give in to his impulses.

His feet moved forward and his hands slipped up her rib cage. "Forward," he murmured, his lips nearly touching her ear. He brought her back and his hands inched down, his fingers gently stroking her hips. His words were husky. "We just go back and forth, back and forth, building momentum until we finally slip the surly bonds of earth."

"But Morgan," Jolie protested breathlessly, his words and his actions taking their toll, "we're not even moving."

"A minor detail," he whispered into her hair.

"But, Morgan," she croaked, "by its very definition, *swinging* implies some form of movement."

"Do you want to?"

The question was loaded with innuendo. Jolie slid off the swing and into his arms. Her plan was to put an end

75

to this risky business, but instead Morgan sat on the swing and pulled her into his lap. Wrapping her in the security of his strong arms, he said, "Swinging double is twice the fun. I'll show you."

It had been a long time since swinging had been this exciting. Jolie had never felt so safe, so warm, so protected. At the same time, the onslaught of such feelings dismayed her. She didn't need protection; she didn't want the dubious safety of a man's arms around her. "We're still not swinging."

"Hold on, lady. I'm about to give you the swing of your life." Morgan's feet pushed them back rapidly until they were airborne. Then he leaned far back, his long legs outstretched.

Jolie gasped as the sudden force thrust her body against the virile strength of him. An elemental fear of falling prompted her to lock her legs around his. The ebb and flow of the star-dusted sky filled her vision, and the rumbling vibration of Morgan's rich laughter filled her senses. She experienced the nostalgic exhilaration of childhood as the soft night breeze riffled her hair.

They were alone in the yard, perhaps in the whole world, and she found herself laughing joyously.

So she *could* laugh, he thought happily. The tinkling sound of it thrilled Morgan, and he felt inordinately proud of himself for being responsible for it. If being flung through the air on a swing could make her happy, she'd be delirious before he was finished with his pursuit of her. He tightened his arms around her.

Jolie choked off her laughter and stiffened in his arms, suddenly aghast at her own lack of inhibition. Too fast, she told her swirling senses—not only the movement of the swing, but also the intensity of the feelings that had come over her so quickly, feelings for a man she scarcely knew.

"Morgan, this is fun, but I'm afraid we're going to fall."

"You just may be right, Jolie," he confirmed. He'd already begun the dangerous tumble himself.

He slowed the swing, dragging his feet over soft earth from which the grass had been worn away. He stood her on her feet and faced her, his features shadowed by the moonlight filtering through the trees.

A small part of Jolie challenged him to say or do something, to spoil the mood, to do anything that would make him less than perfect.

But instead Morgan put his arm around her shoulders and they walked back to the deck. It felt so right, so natural to curl her arm around his waist.

"You know, you're the first woman I've ever swung with," he confided with false innocence.

Jolie grinned, once again caught up in his zany mood. "I wouldn't care to bet any money on that one."

"Okay. I'll rephrase that: You are the first woman I've ever been on a swing with."

"It was a first for me too."

In a comically inept Bogie imitation, Morgan promised, "Stick with me, kid, and I'll make sure this is only the first of many firsts." He didn't dare tell her how important she was becoming to him. He didn't dare do what he wanted to do, so he hid his overwhelming emotions behind his smile.

They sat on the chairs outside and watched the clouds float across the face of the moon. "Is there someone special in your life, Jolie? I need to know."

"Not anymore."

"What about Meggie's father? What role does he play in your life?" Bad mistake, he realized too late as he watched her features rearrange themselves into a closed expression. For some reason this was not something she wanted to talk about. It was, however, something he needed to know.

"Meggie's father plays no part in our lives." Jolie felt a trembling inside—not for any emotion evoked by the

77

mention of Stephen; she was over that. It was the undisguised interest Morgan showed in her. Part of her was flattered, pleased and delighted that such an attractive man found her interesting. Yet another part cursed the circumstances that made her afraid to fall in love.

Falling in love? Was that what was happening? Was that why she felt alive for the first time in years? Was it that easy?

"Are you saying that he doesn't even visit her?"

"That's right."

"Where does he live? The moon? I can't believe any man wouldn't want Meggie to be part of his life."

"He lives in Dallas. Stephen has no interest in his daughter. He's never accepted her." Jolie hadn't meant to become emotional but she couldn't keep the pain out of her voice. "He couldn't handle having a child that was less than perfect, one he didn't think could live up to his expectations—a child that he felt was inadequate to carry on the venerated name of Meredith."

"Meredith?"

Jolie's smile was without mirth. "I see you've heard of the famous Dallas Merediths. I'm not surprised. Everyone has. O'Day was my maiden name. After the divorce I took it back and had Meggie's name legally changed."

Morgan could sense the anger, bitterness and regret that underscored her words. There was more than she was willing to tell right now, but he could wait for the rest. He wouldn't push her.

He could already see her easing shut the doors that had opened between them. He cursed himself for bringing up a sore subject and ruining the closeness they'd established. But most of all, he cursed himself for putting that wounded look back into her eyes. That had never been part of his plan; he wanted only to make her happy.

He reached out and held her face lightly. She noticed a subtle softness in his expression, and in a perverse way she was glad he'd brought up the unhappy topic of her previous marriage. It had helped her ease back from that dangerous ledge of vulnerability.

"Don't shut me out, Jolie," Morgan whispered. "You have to let go of the past. You can't let it spoil the present, and I hope you won't let it prevent the future from being all that it can be. Let me help you get rid of it."

"I'm rid of it already." She couldn't admit that the hurt and anger were still a little sharp around the edges. They always would be. But his words were as soft and soothing as the night breeze on her face.

"I want to help you heal the wound."

"Don't offer me Band-Aids, Morgan, when you don't even understand the extent of the injury."

He recoiled, and she knew she'd hurt him. But she just couldn't let him any closer. It would be better to get him off the determined course he had set, a course aimed at baring all her secrets. She turned the focus of the conversation on him. "I have a question for you," she said with false brightness.

"I have nothing to hide."

"Who is the mysterious Monica your aunt Nevada felt I needed to find out about at dinner?" There. It was out. If he wanted to get personal it was better for him to be the object of discussion.

Morgan was astute enough to understand what Jolie was trying to do. As he saw it, he had two options. He could continue to pursue his line of questioning and risk losing her, or he could let it pass and try to recapture their earlier mood.

He smiled engagingly. "Just someone I know. Why do you ask?"

"I got a different impression. She must be very important for your aunt to keep bringing her up."

"Maybe she's only important to my aunt."

This was much safer ground, and Jolie allowed herself the luxury of a teasing smile. "I suspect you're seeing her

79

now and are just trying to play fast and loose with my affections while she is safely out of town."

"Why, madam, you wound me," he said dramatically as he feigned a shocked look. "I never play loose—just fast."

"Well, I don't even play."

"Too bad. Obviously you've never had the right playmate." He glanced at the moon. "Yep, too bad. This night was made-to-order for romance."

"I'm not looking for romance."

"How about a meaningless, superficial affair?"

She shook her head, barely suppressing her laughter. "Not that either." She couldn't decide if his physical appeal enhanced his humor or vice versa. She tugged him to his feet and savored the warmth of his hand. "I think you'd better go home before your suggestions degenerate any further."

Under the yellow glow of the front porch light, Morgan turned to Jolie. When he would have taken her into his arms, she inched away, hesitant to allow him to initiate another kissing session.

"I think we've been friendly enough for one night," she demurred. "No more kisses."

"What's a few kisses between friends?"

"The difference between remaining friends and becoming something more."

"In that case, how about a hug for the road."

He had a way with words, she'd give him that. But Jolie didn't protest as he wrapped her in a tender embrace. She knew a sincere request would bring her instant release, but she couldn't bring herself to voice one. Her arms curled around his waist, and Morgan pulled her closer.

"Ah, Jolie," he whispered. "My sweet lady." The words he sighed against her hair made her want to yield to the burning sweetness held captive within her.

The simple hug became a whirlpool of sensations.

There was the strong feel of him, so healthy and male; the woodsy scent of his after-shave, subtle yet spicy. As she inhaled, the erotic aroma seemed to penetrate her control, to dissolve her resistance.

He held her tightly in his arms, and her slender body was engulfed by his powerful one, making her feel sheltered and warm. He filled all her empty spaces—spaces that hadn't even seemed empty until she met Morgan.

"It's meant to be." His lips brushed her temple. "And it will be."

Jolie rested her forehead on his chest, struggling to control her erratic breathing. He stroked her hair and rested his cheek against the top of her head.

His voice was a tremulous whisper. "Was it as good for you as it was for me?" Then he chuckled, breaking the sensual thread. "Please keep in mind, when you answer, that the male ego is a fragile thing."

Jolie giggled and buried her face against his chest where she could feel his heart beating furiously. He was certifiably nuts. Either that or he was so finely atuned to her feelings that he instinctively knew when to ease up. "It wasn't bad. You're a good hugger."

"So are you." His fingers were still gently stroking her hair. "You aren't just saying that to make me feel good, are you?"

Jolie laughed, pushing him away. "No, I'm not just saying that."

"Good." He breathed dramatically. "When can I see you again?"

"Morgan—"

"And I mean on a *real* date. Tonight was not a genuine representation of what I have to offer. Although it did have its moments."

Jolie found it difficult to keep her inspired fantasizing at bay when he said that. "Tonight was . . . tonight was nice, but . . ." Her voice trailed away.

"But?"

"I'm not looking for love and I'm not interested in fooling around."

"No problem," he assured her. "I can do it for both of us."

She kissed her fingertips and touched his lips gently. "Good night, Morgan."

"Is that it?" he asked incredulously.

"I'm afraid so," she informed him in a singsong, teasing voice. It did feel good to be lighthearted. In a sudden burst of realization, it occurred to her that Morgan Asher was the only man she'd ever met who was capable of making her feel that way. "Isn't that the way friends say good night?"

"No, it needs work," he improvised.

Caressing her with his eyes, Morgan longed to take her into his arms and kiss her the way she needed to be kissed.

"I can be patient," he warned. "But I think you and I both know that we are destined for more than friendship. From the first moment I saw you, I knew you were special. That *we* were special." No harm in giving her something to think about, and, he hoped, something to dream about.

"I think you'd better go now," she murmured, and stepped back into the lonely safety of her home.

CHAPTER SIX

Monday was the slowest day of the week. It was the day
Jolie usually spent trying to catch up on the backlog of
paperwork she allowed to accumulate during the other,
busier days. She'd cleared a space in the middle of her
overloaded desk and was hunched over a state sales tax
form. An overdue state sales tax form, she reminded herself.

It was times like these when she was sorry that she had
worked so hard for her business degree. If only she'd had
the foresight to study psychology or literature, she could
have farmed out such tedious tasks with a clear con-
science. As it was, she was stuck with the job.

She'd always been able to tune out the sounds around
her, to focus her full attention on the task at hand. The
pot banging from the kitchen, the heavy-metal music
from Sharon's radio, even the good-natured kibitzing
among the staff could easily be relegated to the status of
white noise, ever present but not unduly distracting.

As she added a column of figures for the third time and
arrived at yet a different sum, she realized that her attention was definitely divided today.

"Got a minute?" Sharon's bright head poked around
the door. Without waiting for an answer, she came in and
set a cup of coffee and one of Mrs. Lemmons's mouth-
watering croissants in front of Jolie.

"What's this? I didn't know we had curb service."

Sharon pulled up a folding chair and braced her elbows on Jolie's carefully penciled ledger sheets. "Just a little something to loosen your tongue."

"About what?" Jolie asked suspiciously.

"About last night," Sharon said patiently. "Come on. Details."

"I've told you about dinner, about Morgan's family and—"

"The house and the animals," Sharon interrupted. "Yes, yes, I know but I want to hear about *him*. Is the man as sexy as he looks?"

They had these conversations all the time. Sharon seemed to relish exploring all the possibilities of male-female relationships. The problem was that before it had always been Sharon's relationships they'd explored.

"He's charming," Jolie hedged.

"Charming? What's that mean? The way the sparks were flying between you two yesterday, I expected you to be nursing some pretty serious burns this morning."

Jolie couldn't afford to encourage Sharon. Even a pat on the head would be grist for her mill. "Nothing happened."

"Nothing?" she said in a loud, incredulous tone.

"Nothing." That wasn't exactly true, but Jolie managed to keep her voice as innocent as her expression.

"He did kiss you, didn't he?"

"We shared a—brief, friendly kiss," Jolie admitted.

"Aha! You sounded wistful just then. You were touched by him." Sharon's smug look said even more. "Didn't he try anything?"

Jolie gave Sharon a how-could-you-ask-such-a-thing look and sipped her coffee with studied nonchalance. She was torn between telling her best friend how incredibly romantic her evening had been and wanting to keep it to herself, hugging the warm secret to her heart a little longer.

"Doesn't that upset you?" Sharon goaded.

"What?"

"Well, if a man like Morgan Asher didn't try something with me, I'd be rushing out to buy a truckload of breath mints."

"I really hadn't thought about it." What a fabrication! Morgan Asher was all she'd been able to think about after she closed her door last night. Even at this moment the mere thought of that man did things to her body she could only marvel at. She was elementally, physically, primitively attracted to him.

So what was she going to do about it? Nothing. Absolutely, positively nothing.

"Jolie?" Sharon demanded.

"What?" She asked crossly.

"I said, are you going to see him again?"

"I don't think so."

"Well, maybe that's for the best. What you need is someone like Sven: a warm-blooded male animal who can raise your hormone levels. I think it has something to do with those long, cold Scandinavian winters."

"Sharon, don't you have some omelets to beat or something?"

The redhead got up and took her leave. "Okay, okay," she said over her shoulder. "Never let it be said that Sharon Connelly can't take a hint."

Jolie wadded a piece of paper and pitched it at her friend's back. Leave it to Sharon to get right to the heart of the matter.

Her concentration was shot. How could she be expected to pay attention to monotonous clerical work when thoughts of Morgan Asher kept intruding? The more she tried not to think about him, the more insistent his image became.

She had come up with a dozen reasons she shouldn't see him, none of them convincing. The net result was that she found him more fascinating than before. The very things that should have discouraged her—his eccentric-

85

ity, his off-beat way of looking at the world—only intrigued her more.

She couldn't deny what she felt for him but even that went beyond the dazzling smile, the twinkling blue eyes, the just-so perfection of his face and form. It even went beyond the way he made her feel when they touched. She sensed a power in Morgan Asher, and despite the warnings of her gun-shy heart, she found herself wanting to know that power more intimately.

She tried to tell herself that his lack of seriousness made him too much like Stephen Meredith, but even she wouldn't believe it. There seemed to be none of Stephen's selfishness, irresponsibility or faithlessness in Morgan. But did she really know that? She only sensed it, only wanted to believe it, she chided herself, and last night she had been tempted to give in to it.

She had enough to keep her busy in the office all day, and if she bolted the door, maybe she could avoid any more of Sharon's interrogations. She went back to work, but a scream from the kitchen caused her head to snap up in alarm.

She pushed back her chair and made a mad dash through the quiet restaurant. She shouldered open the swinging kitchen doors and found chaos.

The scream had come from Mrs. Lemmons, who was normally voluble and given to fits of temperament befitting an artiste. But she was such a good cook, she could probably make library paste appetizing, so Jolie had made it a policy to overlook her outbursts.

But now the large, gray-haired woman was ranting in a fashion no one could ignore. Her arms waving wildly, her ample bosom heaving, she directed her tirade at Sharon.

Sharon was blitzing the large kitchen with an out-of-control fire extinguisher in one hand and fending off the distraught cook with the other. Willard, their aged dishwasher and busboy, was beside himself with laughter, while Amy, the part-time student waitress, was wide-eyed and speechless.

"What is going on in here?" Jolie shouted above the melee.

"I think I just saved us from certain destruction," Sharon answered with an immodest gleam in her eyes.

"I can see that."

"You adle-pated booby!" Mrs. Lemmons shouted at the redhead. "Look at my croissants! Look at my quiches, my muffins!" Her wild gesture took in the array of baked goods she'd placed on warming trays in anticipation of their first customers. The food was heavily dusted with the chalky white residue from the extinguisher.

Jolie turned to Sharon, who seemed surprised that her act of heroism was to go unpraised. "What happened?"

"I walked in and found the kitchen in blazes. Being quick-witted and fast on my feet, I pulled out the trusty fire extinguisher and saved the day." She stated her case.

"In blazes, you say?" Mrs. Lemmons screeched. "Girl, now I know you don't have both oars in the water." She turned to the counter and picked up a charred potholder. "This is what was on fire. This itty-bitty old potholder that I left too close to the burner. A raging inferno it ain't!" The prosecution rested.

Sharon had the good grace to look abashed.

"This"—Jolie's arms swept around the debacle—"all this was to save us from a blazing potholder?"

The guilty party shifted her weight uneasily from one foot to the other, then began her defense. "Well-ll-ll, it looked like a big fire when I walked in on it. There was smoke and everything."

"But not enough to set off the smoke alarms?" Jolie objected.

"Didn't have time," Mrs. Lemmons accused. "Sparky the Wonder Girl was too fast on the draw."

"Reckon we maybe oughta get one of them newfangled

extinguishers that just takes the oxygen outta the air. Leastwise, that way we'd still be able to serve the food." Willard stopped laughing long enough to insert his judgment. The elderly man looked from woman to woman and, finding himself outnumbered, went back to rolling silverware in napkins.

"Willard is right," Jolie said. "We should have replaced that dry chemical extinguisher long ago." It hadn't been a good week, she thought before she recalled that it was only Monday. She surveyed the mess and the ruined food.

"There's enough white stuff in here to crash land a crippled seven forty-seven." Jolie started laughing and couldn't stop. This should be a serious crisis. She should be worried about how they would feed their customers. She should be concerned with how the lost revenues would cut into their profit margin.

But she wasn't. All she could think of was what a kick Morgan would get out of this whole episode. It *was* funny, and since she'd met him she could appreciate the absurdity of it.

She poked the toasted potholder and choked back more laughter, causing tears of mirth to fill her eyes. "Now what do we do?"

"Punt," said Mrs. Lemmons. She was a devoted Sooners fan.

"Could you whip up another batch of muffins?" Jolie asked, testing the waters.

"Reckon so. We got enough eggs to make omelets if you put out a special on 'em and push 'em. I can bake some more quiches and croissants before the lunch crowd arrives, but the brunch bunch will have to settle for omelets and crepes."

Jolie nodded. The woman was a marvel of organization. They were lucky to have such a treasure. "Sounds good to me, Mrs. Lemmons. Sharon, will you put up the sign announcing today's special? Since it's Monday, I doubt we'll be deluged with customers."

Amy, who'd stepped out when the excitement was over, dashed back into the kitchen. Her eyes were even wider than before. "Jolie, take a look in the dining room." She thrust a stack of orders at Mrs. Lemmons.

Jolie, with Sharon at her heels, poked her head through the swinging door. The little plant-filled tearoom was bursting with patrons.

"Where did they all come from?" Sharon wanted to know.

"Beats me. Maybe being at the Medieval Fair is going to really pay off. Maybe we just needed that extra added exposure."

There were many new faces among their regular coffee and croissant customers and Jolie recognized two of them as the couple who had so kindly helped her look for Meggie. A crowded dining room would normally be a godsend. With the food shortage today, it was just another instance of bad timing.

"Hi, Jolie," boomed a familiar baritone. "What's good today?"

She wheeled around and stared into the big blue eyes of Morgan Asher. "What are you doing here?" she cried in dismay.

"That's not a very gracious thing to say to a paying customer," he scolded teasingly. "Especially one who sent so much business your way."

So he was responsible for the extra people she couldn't feed. She might have known. "What did you have to do? Call in a few IOUs?"

What had he done wrong? It had taken two cold showers last night before he could relax, and then he hadn't been able to sleep for thinking about her.

"No. This morning, in the faculty lounge, I just happened to mention that I knew of a great little place for brunch. I guess some of my colleagues got hungry. Professors do get hungry, you know." There was no mistaking that hungry look in his eyes.

During all her daydreams about him, not once had he showed up at her business. Before she could form an appropriate retort to his last statement, Amy was at her side, whispering frantically that they couldn't fill the orders she'd taken.

Jolie and Sharon spent the next few minutes moving from table to table, explaining that due to a mishap in the kitchen they would be unable to serve quiche or croissants. She wondered if they could be accused of illegal bait-and-switch tactics.

She kept a wary eye on Morgan, who seemed content to sip his coffee and watch her. She would have to forget her bookkeeping for a while; she was needed to help serve the unprecedented Monday crowd.

"Is there anything I could do to help?"

Jolie spun around and found Morgan lounging against the counter. "We're kind of busy back here."

"No kidding."

"I can't talk to you right now."

"I didn't ask you to. I asked if I could help out."

"You probably aren't certified."

"Certified as what?"

"By the health department. I could get in big trouble if you touch the food."

Morgan smiled, and suddenly the hectic day didn't seem so bad at all. Everything slowed down and Jolie was caught up in the look of intimacy he gave her, a look that caused her pulse to pick up speed. How could he do that with just a look?

"I wouldn't want you to get in trouble. Can I touch the dirty dishes? Maybe I could help your bus—er—boy clear the tables. He looks as though he could use some help. He's probably the oldest busboy I've ever seen."

He was right about dear old Willard needing some assistance. "Here, put this on and get out there." She tossed

90

him a big white apron. She ached to tie it around his slim waist herself but fought the impulse by stuffing her hands in her pockets. "And try not to break too many."

The door swung shut, but as it flapped open briefly, she caught a glimpse of the handsome man heading for a newly vacated table, a large plastic tub in one hand and a clean towel in the other.

What was he up to? Why did he have to be so unpredictable? It was like him to just appear, throwing her even further out of kilter. While arranging plates on a tray for Amy, she couldn't help thinking what a dashing busboy he made.

Even with all the excitement of the crazy morning, she hadn't failed to notice how attractively Ivy League he looked in his tailored khaki slacks and plaid sport shirt, a navy sweater knotted casually over his shoulders. He must have dressed for class, she decided; he even had on socks.

No doubt he set a lot of coed hearts aflutter, and she wondered how many of his female students actually liked history. The opportunity to sit and stare at Professor Asher three times a week was probably worth suffering through the War of the Roses.

Later, during the lull between brunch and lunch, Morgan joined Jolie in the kitchen. "If the bottom ever falls out of academia, do you think I have a career in dishwashing?"

He poured himself a cup of coffee and eased into a chair at the small table that was set aside for staff meals. He was impressed by Jolie and Sharon's operation. The tearoom was charming, the food delicious and the service efficient. He couldn't understand why he hadn't discovered the place before.

Why had fate kept him and Jolie apart until now? And why the hell wasn't fate cooperating now that they had met?

"I'd be happy to give you a letter of recommendation

91

the next time you apply for a dishwashing position," Jolie said, smiling. "If I didn't know better I'd say that you had previous experience."

"At K.P.? You obviously didn't get a look at my kitchen after the Great Chicken Holocaust last night. Georgia uses every pot in the house, and the fallout from one of her culinary adventures is not a pretty sight."

Her smile became a bigger grin. "I guess Leah and Daniel took care of everything for you. Nonetheless, I'm impressed with your skills in the kitchen."

"Maybe I'll get a chance to impress you with my skills in other rooms someday." She looked so good, he thought. Her face was flushed from the heat of the kitchen and her shining hair was curling slightly around her face where moisture had teased it out of the smooth page boy. She wore a pretty print shirtwaist, and the apricot color brought out all the golden tones of her skin.

Wanting her was a physical ache and he didn't know how much longer he could act casual. Casual? He didn't know how much longer he could act sane.

"Don't you have a class or something?" Jolie read the blatant appraisal in his eyes and wondered what he was thinking. She was just no good at being the object of a man's interest. Why couldn't she bat her eyelashes and give as good as she got?

"Casting me aside now that I've worked my fingers to the bone for you?"

She met his steady blue gaze and felt the electricity arc across the table. She shifted in her chair with the hope of putting a few more millimeters of empty air between them.

"I just thought you might have something else to do."

His rolling chuckle sounded again, and he looked at the slim gold watch on his wrist. "Actually I do have a class in a little while. On Mondays my graduate assistants take the morning freshman discussion groups. I guess I should get to my office and go over my notes for the upperclassmen."

Jolie breathed a deep sigh of relief that he would soon be on his way. She hadn't felt normal since the first time she'd laid eyes on him. "Thanks for helping out. You always seem to be around when I need rescuing."

"That's a knight's primary occupation, you know. Rescuing beautiful damsels in distress."

"Yes, well, hopefully I can get through the rest of the week without requiring your services again."

Morgan slapped his thigh. "Shucks, just when I was beginning to get the hang of it, too."

Jolie looked at him and sighed. "Are you ever serious?"

"God, I hope not. Life's too serious to be taken seriously."

She stood, extending her hand. A handshake was an act of dismissal. She was eager for Morgan Asher to take his unbelievably blue eyes and leave so she could think straight again. If that were possible.

Instead of shaking her hand, he raised it to his lips, brushing it gently. The gesture sent a tremor through her arm that probably registered somewhere on somebody's Richter scale.

Still holding her hand, he said, "I'd like to see you again, Jolie. Will you go out with me?"

She swallowed. "You mean on a date?"

"Unless you can think of something better."

"I should have told you last night. I don't date; that is, I have dated, but I don't date now. And I don't think I could, so I guess not," she ended lamely. He made her feel like a kindergartner on her first day of school. What had happened to the cool, aloof facade she'd perfected over the years?

She knew the answer.

Morgan had melted it like a snowflake in a firestorm.

"What about last night?" he persisted, hoping that she

93

really wanted to say yes. Why was she compelled to deny herself?

"Last night?" she stalled. "That was different. Meggie was there, your mother . . ."

"And we weren't alone?"

"Exactly. It wasn't *really* a date."

"True," he agreed grudgingly. "Is it the concept of dating in general you oppose or is it me specifically?"

He hadn't let go of her hand and she wondered if she should forcibly withdraw it. "It's just that I'm very busy and Meggie and the restaurant seem to take up most of my time and energy. I find I don't have time to develop social relationships." There. That sounded pretty good. Hadn't she read that in a woman's magazine once?

"Hmmm. Social relationships? That sounds like more fun than just dating. I'd like to try that." She was the most refreshingly prim woman he'd ever met. It would be a challenge to awaken the sexuality sleeping beneath her ladylike exterior. "I guess you're not familiar with the Crusader's Credo?"

"Doesn't it involve sugar lumps?"

"That's only part of it. It's well known that rescued damsels must grant their rescuer an evening of their company."

"I've never heard that before."

"It's widely accepted by the scholarly community. To deny the knight's attention could wreak a horrible metamorphosis in said knight."

Jolie felt like laughing, so she gave in to the feeling. "Oh? Such as?"

"He might turn into a frog." He leaned forward. "Rib-it. Rib-it." Morgan's grin stole her breath away and Jolie knew she was sunk. It was hopeless; she couldn't deny her feelings for him, and she could no longer deny him.

"I thought that only happened to princes."

"That's what they want you to think," he whispered as though imparting a well-kept secret.

94

"They who?" Jolie persisted skeptically.

She could tell by the look on his face that she had set herself up once again. "Why, frogs, of course. The only way they get any action is to mislead poor girls into thinking they're under a spell."

Jolie shook her head. "I think you are certifiable."

"Maybe, but don't tell my fairy godmother, okay? She thinks I'm cute."

"I think—"

"Don't tell me. Let's save some surprises for Saturday night. I'll pick you up at seven thirty. Be on time, because I hate to wait." He pulled her hand to his lips once more.

Before she could speak, before she could refuse or demur, Morgan was gone. She was glad because she knew she couldn't have managed more than a feeble protest at best. She wanted to see him again, alone, without the eyes of curious relatives on them.

When she thought of being alone with him, of touching him and being touched by him, a strange feeling swept through her. She recognized the same exhilaration she'd experienced during her first plane ride. A soaring feeling of power and wonder had engulfed her as the earth fell away and the clouds enveloped her. Being with Morgan Asher was like that. He was a joyride to end all joyrides.

"What was that all about?" Sharon slid into the chair Morgan had just vacated, and Jolie wondered idly if she'd been watching for his departure. "He's such a hunk! What were the two of you laughing and giggling about?"

"Anyone ever tell you what a nosy woman you are, Connelly?"

"Sure. But I never pay attention to them. Sticks and stones and all that. When are you seeing him again?"

"What makes you think I'm going to see him again? You know how I feel about dating."

"I know you turn down every man who asks you out. I know you play the Ice Queen with any male gutsy enough to pay attention to you. I know you've placed yourself in some weird kind of sexual exile since that fink Stephen ran out on you. What I don't know is why. Why let one rotten potato ruin a whole barrelful of potential lovers?"

"Sharon! If you don't mind, I'd rather not discuss my love life in public."

"You mean your lack of one, don't you? No, no, really. I have this theory. I've thought about it a lot and I think I've got you all figured out. Want to hear what I think?"

"No!" Jolie got up and headed for her office, but Sharon doggedly followed.

"My theory is that you're like Sleeping Beauty."

"Right. I pricked my finger on a spinning wheel and fell asleep for a hundred years."

"No. Well, yes, kind of. See, Stephen was like the spinning wheel. You didn't prick your finger on him but you damn near splintered your heart. You didn't fall asleep but you've been walking around in a sexual coma for three years."

"Sharon, I don't want to have this conversation." Jolie picked up the ledgers and feigned concentration. She'd attempted over the years to explain her feelings to her bubbly friend, but they didn't seem to operate on the same wavelength, possibly because Sharon had never known the real heartbreak of a man's rejection.

"Wait, I'm not through yet. This is the best part."

"Sharon, give me a break," Jolie pleaded.

"I figure all you need is Prince Charming to come along, kiss you, and your drowsy little libido will snap right out of it. Just like that." She snapped her fingers for emphasis.

"Just like that?" Jolie imitated the gesture. "You know, Connelly, you're proof of the old saying that a little knowledge is a dangerous thing. That is the most ridiculous thing I've ever heard. Wait—it transcends ridiculous. It's metaphorically absurd." Jolie shook her head to emphasize just how much she didn't believe a word of it.

"Of course, after the handsome prince wakes you up, the two of you will live happily ever after." Sharon leaned back in the folding chair, proud of her cockeyed psychological evaluation.

"Of course. But what if the handsome prince is really an enchanted frog and when I kiss him he turns all green and warty?" Jolie was still thinking about the conversation she'd had with Morgan.

"There were no enchanted frogs in Sleeping Beauty, were there?"

"Never mind. As far as theories go, yours is as good as anyone's. In fact, why don't you write a new pop psychology self-help book? You could call it the Metaphysical Fairy Tale Principle."

"Make fun. You just don't want to face facts. You couldn't find a more likely Prince Charming than Morgan if you called Central Casting." Sharon looked wounded and took a drink of the coffee Jolie had brought into the office with her.

"Or better yet, call it I'm Okay, You're a Frog. That has a nice ring to it."

When it came, Sharon's smile was smug and self-satisfied. "You're going out with him, aren't you? You're trying too hard to avoid the subject."

"Yes, Mom, I'm going out with Morgan. We have a real live date set for Saturday night. Will you be satisfied with a detailed written report or shall I wire myself for sound?"

Sharon considered it. "An oral report is fine. Do you want me to take care of Meggie Muffin for you?"

"Thanks, but Barbara Thompson has been after me to let Meggie spend the night with her and Ryan. I guess I might as well take her up on her offer."

"Great. I'll be over first thing Sunday morning and you can give me a full briefing."

97

"You do that."

"On second thought, I won't come over *too* early. I'd hate to walk in on anything lurid."

"There's two chances of that happening: slim and nonexistent." Jolie spoke with a resolution she didn't wholly feel.

"Don't sell yourself so short, Jolie." Sharon pushed back her chair and headed for the dining room. Snapping her fingers in glee, she whooped as she flounced out the door. "All right! This is gonna be good!"

She was probably going to set up a pool to see who got closest to guessing the exact time Jolie's libido would be awakened. If she wasn't such a good friend, Jolie thought, she might kill her.

She settled back down to work, trying once more to concentrate on the tax report. This time she was distracted by images of frogs with twinkly blue eyes.

CHAPTER SEVEN

Morgan, it seemed, was never on time. He was disgustingly early.

When Jolie answered the door at five minutes past seven, in her robe with her head full of electric curlers, she'd expected to find Sharon. When she saw Morgan she groaned and tried to shut the door in his face. "Go away. Come back in twenty-five minutes."

He grinned around the door jamb through which he had inserted his foot. "You really should work on your greetings. If I didn't know better, I'd think you weren't glad to see me."

Jolie sighed resolutely and opened the door. Why should she be surprised by this Morgan-like unpredictability? "You need to work seriously on your timing."

But that was all he needed to work on, she noticed with appreciation as he strode into the living room. Everything else was perfect.

He wore tailored gray slacks, a navy blazer and an open-necked white silk shirt as effortlessly as he'd worn faded jeans. Whether crusader or sophisticate, he was always pulling the rug out from under her.

Morgan regarded the curlers Jolie was worrying self-consciously with amusement. "Can you pick up Topeka on those things?"

She threw him a withering look and began snatching

them out. "The sexes will never truly be equal until men become as dependent on beauty aids as women."

She didn't need beauty aids, he thought as he took in the fresh, sweet smell of her hair and the unfettered curves under her thin robe. This breathless deshabille suited her far better than the restrained propriety she usually adopted. And it was a lot more tempting.

She was right. He should leave now and come back when she had donned her armor of primness. Finding her mussed and out of uniform was dangerous. "I didn't come early to embarrass you. I'm early because I was eager to see you again. It's been five days." Plus seven hours and fifteen minutes, he added silently.

He seemed nonplussed by his own admission. Jolie's frown softened around the edges and her heart assumed the alarming pace it usually kept when he was around. "I just hate for you to see me like this."

If she looked any better than she did right now, he thought, he couldn't be held responsible for his actions. "Don't worry about it. You should see me first thing in the morning. I look like a lumberjack before spring thaw."

"Humph." Jolie doubted if he could ever look anything less than wonderful. "I'd have to see that to believe it."

There was a smug gleam in his eye as he cast his line and reeled her in. "That can be arranged. Anytime you're ready, just say the word."

Would she always be his straight man? Why couldn't she see it coming? Because, she pointed out to herself, he totally boggled her senses. Cheeks aflame, Jolie flounced into her bedroom and slammed the door.

When she finally reentered the living room, the look of pure male appreciation on Morgan's face made her glad she'd borrowed the slinky black sheath from Sharon. It had threadlike straps that bared her shoulders and a tulip hemline that revealed a bit too much leg. It made her feel daring.

Excitement had nibbled at her poise all day, and now Morgan's intimately assessing look posed an even greater threat to her aplomb.

His gaze was hypnotic. She had to fight a now-familiar craving to have his hands mold her body to his masculine length. Damn the man and his compelling eyes. At times they were like the mirror-smooth surface of a lake, reflecting calm and assurance. At others they twinkled with devilment and wry humor. She wondered if they sparkled like blue ice when he was angry. At this moment they seemed shadowed by what could only be unveiled longing.

"I hope I'm dressed appropriately," she ventured. "You didn't say where we were going." It was impossible to second-guess him, and for all she knew they could be headed for the wrestling matches or a picnic at the lake.

"You're perfect," he said as he followed her out the door. This sultry Jolie was new, but not totally unexpected. Morgan had known that beneath her cool facade there was a woman capable of formidable passion. A woman he could watch unfold, little by little, like a blossoming rose. A woman he would never grow tired of.

Muldoon's, a small supper club featuring a popular musical trio, had the quintessential romantic atmosphere. Scented candles, lush green plants, soft music and elegant tables added to the ambience. A uniformed waiter showed them to their table near the terrace and presented Jolie with a long-stemmed red rose. Jolie could see a few couples swaying on the outdoor dance floor, where they were soon joined by others for moonlight dancing.

If Morgan was trying to wear down her resistance, he was doing a great job. She hadn't felt so female in a long time.

Morgan leaned across the table after the waiter had left with their orders and took her hand in his. "Is it all right if we hold hands?" he asked, thinking that if he didn't touch her soon he'd burst from the prolonged anticipation of the last five days.

"I suppose so," she said quietly, wishing he wouldn't seek permission each time he touched her, wishing he weren't regarding her so intently. Every time his gaze met hers, her heart turned over in response. Reflexively her right hand rose, covering her heart, and she wondered if he could hear the loud drumming. And if so, did he realize he was the reason that it beat with a crazy rhythm all its own?

His gaze dropped from her eyes to her shoulders, then lower. His desire quickened at the sight of so much creamy skin and he tamped down the urge to tell the waiter to just forget about the food. Forcing his eyes to return to her face, he swallowed twice before he could speak without betraying his emotions.

"Have I told you how beautiful you are?" At her suspicious look, he tightened the fingers holding hers. "I know it's an overused line but I've never used it before. And in your case it's not even a line. I do think you're beautiful."

His magnetism was so potent, his look so sincere, that Jolie even felt beautiful. His mesmerizing eyes riveted her to the spot, and her doubts melted like snow in the warm sunshine of his adoring gaze. "Thank you," she managed lamely.

"Thank *you,*" he insisted.

"For what?"

"For everything." He shrugged, feeling helplessly at a loss for the appropriate words to express his feelings. "For being you, for coming out with me tonight." He shrugged again. "For everything."

Jolie's senses eddied and she felt infused with new life. She had a sudden, overwhelming urge to clamp the rose in her teeth, leap to her feet and do a seductive, hipswaying dance—all for Morgan. Luckily, at that moment the waiter arrived with their wine and salads, and she was saved from making her terpsichorean debut.

"To you, Jolie," Morgan toasted as their glasses clinked. "I'm lucky to have found you."

"And to you, Morgan," she said bravely, honestly. "To us."

She saw the heart-rending tenderness of his gaze as it locked with her own. As they sipped the wine, a smoky, sensuous light seemed to pass between them. As soft as a caress, his roving stare swept lazily over her, giving rise to a more meaningful tingling deep inside her.

Jolie had been ogled more than a few times and could recognize lust in a man's look. Being the recipient of such leers had always made her cringe inside. But everything was different with Morgan. His intent yet gentle scrutiny made her feel all-powerful, all-adored. No man had ever looked at her quite like this before, and she'd never felt quite so wonderful.

"You make me feel good about myself, Morgan."

"Do I?" he smiled, relishing Jolie's forthrightness.

"Yes. And you know it." She hesitated for only a moment before daring to ask, "What do I make you feel?"

Morgan pulled her hand to his lips and caressed it. "If I told you truthfully how you make me feel, you might have me arrested."

Jolie's cheeks felt hot with embarrassment even as she reveled in his blunt answer. "You don't play fair."

"On the contrary," he said, his eyes twinkling rakishly. "You'll find out, when we play, just how fair I can be."

"Are you laughing at me?"

"Never." His expression was one of genuine sincerity. "I made a vow to be honest with you. I'm committed to that vow and I never take commitment lightly."

The waiter's timely arrival let Jolie off the proverbial hook. Morgan was forced to release her hand so they could eat—which was the last thing Jolie wanted to do.

Morgan went through the motions of eating. He observed the social amenities but scarcely tasted the food. He felt a special bond forging between them and he wondered if Jolie was aware yet of its existence.

He watched her fork enviously as it slid from her lips and had to tear his gaze away, chastising himself for his thoughts. "When you were a little girl, did you ever do anything you knew was forbidden but just couldn't resist?"

"Not that I remember. Did you?"

"Sure. But I always weighed the pros and cons of any deed beforehand. If the thrill overbalanced the punishment, I did it."

"Now I know what your mother meant when she said there were reasons she'd only had one child," Jolie said teasingly.

Morgan chuckled. "I was a trial to her, but knowing Georgia, I think she'd have been disappointed if I'd been unimaginative and obedient."

"You've got a point there."

Morgan folded his arms on the table and leaned forward. "Tell me what kind of child you were."

"I was agonizingly shy," she recalled.

"Lots of children are basically timid," he commiserated. "Even I was bashful to an extent."

"I'm not talking your basic timidity here," she said. "I was painfully insecure. It nearly paralyzed me socially."

"How shy were you?" he said playfully.

"I was so shy that on my first day of school I couldn't bring myself to talk. I couldn't even tell the teacher my name. Finally one of the neighbor kids had to tell her."

"That doesn't sound so bad. At least someone knew you and you didn't have to go by Jane Doe."

"Well, it was terrible for me. The child who gave her my name had a speech problem. The teacher called me Jolly all day."

Morgan grinned. "And you let her?"

"I couldn't help it." Jolie smiled ruefully, as only

someone who's overcome a handicap can. "I was afraid to correct the teacher, afraid I would cry if I spoke up, and afraid of attracting even more unwanted attention to myself."

"That's a lot of fear. How did you manage to overcome it?"

"Some of it I outgrew, but after my divorce I took an assertiveness course just to be on the safe side."

Jolie's admissions gave Morgan even more insight into her personality. Anyone who'd borne such a burden of childhood insecurity was sure to have residual adult doubts as well. He wished he'd known her then, so he could have been her boyish champion. How different their growing-up years must have been, he thought.

"I was always pretty aggressive as a child."

"I never doubted it for a moment," Jolie said.

"I had a well-earned reputation as the class clown, and unlike you, I never worried about attracting attention."

"Every teacher's ideal," she said with a smile.

"I wasn't so bad. My biggest problem, as my parents frequently pointed out, was my inability to judge the merits of an idea. I subscribed to the try-everything-at-least-once philosophy even then."

Jolie caught a fleeting glimpse of the boy Morgan had been. He was reflected, for a moment, in the impish gleam in his eyes. "I take it you weren't exactly an armchair philosopher."

"You take it right. Pop always said that if someone had dared me to jump off the roof, I would have jumped."

"Surely not," she scoffed. "What was the biggest dare you ever took?"

Morgan smiled at the memory. "I shouldn't tell you."

"Turnabout is fair play," she insisted. "I told you about Jolly."

"Do you promise not to think badly of me?"

"Promise." She couldn't think bad thoughts about Morgan if she tried. And she had tried.

Morgan chuckled. "Swear it!"

Her eyes narrowed suspiciously. "My, my, what kind of junior grade delinquent were you, anyway? What did you do?"

"Well," he said slowly, "it was a *double* dare. You know how hard those are to resist."

"The very worst kind," she agreed earnestly, enjoying the suspense.

"Let me say up front that it was all Billy Bob Sixkiller's fault."

"Disclaimers before I even hear the story? Who's Billy Bob Sixkiller?"

"Billy Bob was my best friend in the third grade. We were practically brothers. That is, until he caused all the hullabaloo that got my mother drummed out of the garden club." Morgan pursed his lips thoughtfully. "I never forgave him for that one."

"Your mother was drummed out of her garden club? What happened? I'm dying of curiosity."

"It was a rainy Saturday and—"

"I don't want a weather report. Just give the facts, please."

"If you want to hear this story, you'll just have to bear with me. It's all pertinent information," he said with a wicked little grin. "Billy Bob and I were bored, bored, bored. Since it was raining, we couldn't play outdoors. My mother had a club meeting going on downstairs and wouldn't allow us to watch television either. So we hid in the closet trying to overhear some juicy gossip."

"And? Did you hear any?"

"No. Not unless you think the root rot on Mrs. Simpson's begonias was as scandalous as some of those old biddies did. Then Billy Bob thought of something that would set them on their ears." Morgan lowered his voice and Jolie leaned closer to hear the rest.

"What?"

106

"You have to keep in mind that Billy Bob is half Cherokee Indian."

"Okay, okay," she said impatiently.

"He suggested that we 'streak' through the living room where the meeting was taking place. I was to scream, 'The Indians are coming, the Indians are coming, hang on to your scalps,' while he chased me with a toy tomahawk."

"You didn't!"

"I told him there was no way I'd do such a thing."

"Good for you."

"Then he called me a lily-livered, yellow-backed chicken snake in the grass. But I didn't care and I still refused."

"See?" Jolie grinned, knowing full well that he was about to confess his guilt. "I knew you couldn't have been all bad. You were filled with integrity, even as a child."

"Not exactly. He double dared me. What else could I do?"

Jolie laughed delightedly and Morgan was happy to be the instigator of her joy.

Jolie wiped at the tears of mirth in her eyes. "So you took off your clothes and scandalized the sensibilities of all those ladies."

"I was more or less an innocent bystander, but my mother didn't see it that way. I think she was a little upset by the fact that we used her makeup for warpaint. I was grounded for two weeks and Billy Bob wasn't allowed to come over for a month. Harsh woman, my mother."

"I would have paddled your naked behinds," Jolie said in Georgia's defense. "In front of all those women."

Morgan chuckled.

Throughout the rest of the meal they talked and laughed, sharing bits of their lives and making new discoveries about one another. Jolie was startled to find her-

107

self relating stories she'd never told anyone else. She began to feel a warm inner glow of anticipation for the rest of the evening that lay ahead.

Morgan knew if he didn't touch her soon he would go mad with the wanting. Covering her hand with his, he asked, "Did you enjoy the lobster?"

"It was delicious. I've always had a weakness for seafood." And now, she added silently, I have a weakness for your sexy blue eyes, your wacky sense of humor and you.

"Are you ready for the dancing segment of the evening?"

Jolie nodded and they rose together. He placed a warm guiding hand on her bare back and drew her out to the terrace. They clung and swayed, paying scant attention to the tempo of the music.

Morgan's expertise on the dance floor made Jolie's limbs feel as weightless as paper streamers in a breeze. His hands were locked at the base of her spine and burned through the thin material of her dress.

She wrapped her arms around his neck and nestled her cheek against his chest. A small movement brought her even closer to him, and she could feel the erratic cadence of his heart. She felt so right in his arms, as if they were a perfect fit, as though she had always been there. As if she would be there forever.

It seemed that life before Morgan Asher was a dim memory, so completely did he fill her senses. She couldn't recall a time when she hadn't known his comforting strength, his warm affection, his facetious humor. Her rational mind tried to issue warnings, but she disregarded them without hesitation. She preferred to concentrate on the music, the moonlight and the man.

Morgan was an enigma to Jolie. She knew without a doubt that he found her attractive, that he responded to her in much the same way she did to him. She also trusted him not to push her for more than she felt ready to give. She was grateful and bewildered at the same time, and more than a little anxious.

She was ready now—ready for whatever adventure their relationship would become. If he didn't make a move tonight, she would heed Sharon's advice and start shopping for those mints.

Soft lyrics wafted out from the stage. "Two by two, their bodies become one," came the whiskey voice of the woman singer.

Jolie couldn't agree more. She loved the intimacy of dancing with Morgan. She wondered if what they were doing could technically be called dancing. It was more like the vertical expression of a horizontal idea.

Dreamily she wondered what it would be like without music, without the barriers of clothing. Magical. Morgan Asher excited her beyond belief, and she wanted him more than she'd ever wanted another man. What surprised her most was that the thought no longer shocked her.

"Jolie?" he said hoarsely.

"Hmmm?"

"The song is over and the band seems to be leaving." Not that it mattered to him.

She giggled, embarrassed. "I was having so much fun, I didn't even miss them. You're an excellent dancer, Morgan." Reluctantly she untwined her arms, but Morgan kept her in the circle of his embrace.

"Oh," he said, grinning devilishly. "Were we supposed to be dancing?" He winked seductively. "I was holding and swaying."

"And doing a darn nice job of it, too, I might add." Jolie stepped back and he released her.

"Would you like more?" His grin was definitely provocative, intimating a number of exciting possibilities. Dancing wasn't among them.

"I think the place is closing," Jolie pointed out as they made their way, side by side, to their table.

Morgan's hand closed gently on her shoulder and she froze in breathless anticipation of his next words. "Do you have music at your place?" he asked boldly.

What was he really asking? Did it matter? She was beginning to know this man, and what she'd learned about him, she liked. And she wanted him. Knowing that he wanted her, too, made her forget caution. Had she sent Meggie to Barbara's for the night in unconscious preparation for this moment? She had no answers but she knew she couldn't let him leave her tonight—not if he wanted to stay.

"Yes," she said in a breathless whisper.

CHAPTER EIGHT

It was the longest short drive Morgan had ever under-
taken. He thought they'd never arrive. When he'd read
the look in Jolie's eyes at the restaurant, he'd had a prim-
itive urge to throw out his chest and pound it in victory.
She wanted him.

Finally.

When they reached the duplex, Morgan closed the
door and leaned against it, then encircled Jolie in his
arms. "I want to kiss you the way I've been longing to do
since the moment we met," he said in a husky tone.
"Please don't say no. I've waited too long."

"Yes," Jolie breathed. "You have."

His lips met hers for an instant, a butterfly's caress,
before moving to her eyes, her cheek. His tongue traced
the curve of her bottom lip before he placed his mouth
over hers.

Jolie's arms clasped his neck. Her toes dangled a few
inches from the floor as her breasts flattened against his
hard chest. His mouth was hot and sweet and tasted of
the wine they'd shared at dinner. He held her in his powerful arms, pressing her against his chest so she could feel
his wildly hammering heart.

He relaxed and she slid down his body until her feet
touched the floor. She had never understood the term
"thoroughly kissed" until now.

Morgan buried his face in her hair and savored the feel

of her soft curves molding to the contours of his own hard body. He hadn't expected her urgent response. It completely shattered his resolve not to take the undeniable magnetism building between them to its logical conclusion.

He was drunk with the sweetness of her but made himself wait, holding back his own galloping passion until she could catch up with him. He wasn't sure he could control himself much longer now that his world was reduced to need and desire. He sent a fervent message via the fiery possession of her lips.

Jolie felt her knees weaken as his mouth descended again, claiming hers. Deep inside her a dam was breaking, allowing her long-suppressed yearning to flood the banks of her self-control. There would be no more denial, no more waiting. "Shall I turn on the music now? For more dancing?"

"If I'm ever going to leave, it must be now. While I still can, Jolie."

The hesitancy of his words and the question in his voice prompted Jolie to answer with more brave honesty than she'd thought herself capable of. "I don't want you to go, Morgan."

"God knows I don't want to go either. But what little self-command I had when we came in here is long gone."

"I want you to stay, Morgan. I want you . . ."

"If I stay, you know what will happen."

Jolie kissed the tip of his chin. "Yes, I know. I want it to happen." Her fingertips fanned over his chest and slipped behind him to trace concentric circles on his muscled back. "I can hardly wait for it to happen."

He was astounded by her audacity. "Are you sure?"

"Positive." It was too late for choices; she had long passed the point of no return. Jolie knew she was well on her way to loving Morgan. Right or wrong, she could no longer deny it. She didn't even want to try.

She was incredibly light in his arms, more like a child

than a woman. But there was nothing childlike about the undiluted passion burning in her eyes. Or in the way her arms circled his neck, her fingers twining in his hair. He carried her into the bedroom and kicked the door shut with one foot. He wanted to take things slowly. He wanted to savor this once-in-a-lifetime experience.

He wanted to rejoice in every moment he spent with her.

A wonderful feeling of anticipation filled Jolie, creating a knotted tension in the core of her being. She moved to the bedside table and switched on the lotus-shape crystal night light. Almost at once a subtle fragrance was activated and dispersed by the heat from the lamp, filling the room. She'd never realized how seductive the rosy glow of light could be. It cast enough shadows to create a mysterious aura, yet illuminated just enough to titillate the senses.

Morgan stood before her, undressing her in his mind before he did so in reality. After long, charged moments he nudged one thin strap aside with the tip of a finger and dipped his head to kiss the flesh he'd bared. He felt her shudder and he sighed as her head rolled back, inviting him to continue the trail of kisses from her shoulder across her collarbone and on to the other side. He tugged the second strap down with his teeth and kissed her there before drifting down to the swell of her breasts.

Another shudder of pleasure skittered through her as Jolie felt the bodice of her dress slip away, only to be replaced by the silky caress of Morgan's mouth. His lips were warm and soft as he finessed each impatient bud into pebbly arousal. She moaned, arching toward him, her hands finding anchor in his hair when his mouth closed upon her aching breast. She felt his hot tongue exploring, discovering ways to give her new delights.

Morgan was shaken by the power of his emotions, by the aching need he felt for this woman. It thrilled and terrified him at the same time. Never before had touching a woman stimulated him so. As much as he needed her, wanted the fulfillment only she could give him, he drew back.

The next step would have to be hers.

Jolie didn't hesitate. Never had she known such tender wantonness. Her fingers found the buttons of his shirt, and soon it was discarded along with his jacket. She urged him back onto the bed and made quick work of his shoes, socks and trousers.

She smiled appreciatively when he was clad only in the barest black briefs. His legs were sun-browned and firmly muscled and the lamp lit the silky hairs on his arms and legs, making them golden. He was one of those rare men who looked better without clothes, and Jolie was reminded of the classic male figures in ancient art.

She stood before him as he reclined on the bed, watching her with smoldering intensity. Slowly she drew down the zipper of her dress and allowed the garment to whisper to the floor.

Morgan's gasp of delight was clearly audible in the hushed room where their shallow breathing was the only other sound. She was wearing only a scrap of black lace, which clung like a second skin to her breasts and extended down her midriff to end in dainty garters attached to dark stockings. The contrast between her pale skin and the black lace was highly provocative, and Morgan had never seen underwear as wispy as the lacy triangle that barely covered her.

"What do you call that thing you're wearing?" he asked in an emotion-slurred voice.

"It's a bustier."

"How do you get out of it?" His voice rasped.

She planted one foot on the edge of the bed between his knees and freed the silky stocking from the garters. She started to roll the sheer fabric down her leg, but he stopped her.

"Allow me."

114

He completed the task with infinite, maddening deliberation before turning his attention to the other leg. Once the stockings had been discarded, she turned her back to him and lifted her hair, although it wasn't necessary to enable him to undo the hooks. Whether it was unconscious or calculated, the gesture raised his blood pressure to a dangerous level.

He placed his hands on her hips and turned her. Without breaking eye contact, they relieved each other of the final barriers between them. His tanned body seemed to glow in the dim light, and Jolie's heart surged from the sheer joy of just looking at him.

Morgan eased her onto the bed and marveled at her beauty. He slid his palm down the curve of her hip to her thigh and found her skin as soft as satin. He wasn't sure what gave him more pleasure, caressing her or being caressed by her. Deep inside he felt a powerful yearning, and his desire was in full evidence by the time he eased down beside her.

"We'll take it slow and easy," he whispered in her ear. He wasn't at all sure how he was going to make good on that promise. "Don't be nervous."

Her heart was doing aerobics. "That always makes me nervous."

"Making love?" he asked.

"I've usually found that when someone says 'Don't be nervous,' a person should immediately get nervous."

"Not this time," he murmured. Morgan began a delicate seduction of her senses such as Jolie had never experienced before. His pace was incredibly slow, and he set free emotions she hadn't known she possessed.

His hands, his lips were everywhere, discovering every vulnerable spot on her body, making her weak with pleasure, making her moan with delight. Slowly he drove her wild with a tenderness that went far beyond sexual hunger.

He made her head swim with desire and wonder. His

hands never stayed long enough in one place for her to capture the delicious sensations. They brushed across her throbbing breast, skimming the smooth silky skin of her stomach, and drifted lower, bringing a sigh of desperation from deep within her.

His breath quickened in tempo with hers and he felt her skin quiver under his lips as his mouth wandered over the inner curve of her throat, then lower to once again possess the lushness of her breasts. He fought to maintain his control when his hand found her pliant flesh, his gentle massage causing her body to strain against him.

She felt his lashes brush her skin, heard the sigh of a whispered endearment. Then his lips softly rolled back and forth over one distended nipple, and her heart began to pound.

She felt the thud of his pulse when her naked breasts moved against his heated flesh and reveled in the pressure of his hips on her inner thighs. Her hands caught in his hair, pulling his head to hers. Her name was a whispered plea of promised sweetness against her lips. Over and over his mouth seared hers, clouding out the last of any rational thoughts.

"You're shaking," he murmured.

"No, no," she denied breathlessly. She had to stop this trembling. She was a grown woman and well aware of what was about to happen. But something told her she could never imagine anything like what Morgan's lovemaking promised. His lips closed on her breast again and she vaulted against him in a wild shudder of delight.

Morgan let out a shaky sigh and his hands became more demanding. He tantalized her body and thrilled her mind with every touch. And always there was the spiraling, exhilarating escalation of excitement.

Jolie abandoned the last of her inhibitions as she teased, demanded and tantalized Morgan in return.

When finally they were joined it was the perfect, superb melding of one body to its mate. Breathing as one, Jolie and Morgan moved in absolute harmony to a tempo both urgent and savoring. He thrust his hands into her hair, holding her so their eyes locked in the soft glow of the lamp.

"Now," he gasped.

Still holding her eyes with his own, Morgan propelled them both to the tumult. It was a magical place that pulsed and spun for a sweet blissful eternity.

He gathered her by the shoulders and rolled over, taking her trembling body with him, holding her next to his heart.

"Jolie O'Day, you're *my* lady now," he whispered.

Still breathless and spent, Jolie couldn't speak. She lay her cheek against his shoulder and tried to steady her racing heart. Although the urgency had waned, the excitement was still alive and pulsating inside her. She felt almost brave and a little giddy with the awakening of her sexual self. She had just made exquisite love with a most compelling man whom she'd known for only a week. But never had anything felt so right.

He held her in silence for a long time. Finally, when he sensed her relaxing, when her breathing had returned to normal, he spoke. "You're part of me now, Jolie. Trust me enough to know you, to know your past. Trust me enough to share yourself with me. You've given me your body. Please give me your trust."

As he held her, she talked. She told him that she'd been reared by her mother after her father left one day and never returned. She told him how she'd sat with her mother, too young to understand, too overwhelmed to offer solace, and listened to her mother lament the man she loved.

Jolie had always thought it was her fault her father had left them, and she'd been an adult before she'd given up that frightening idea.

Her mother never remarried, never overcame the loss

of her one true love. Her father took care of them finan-
cially, but Jolie had little contact with him as she grew
up. He died without a reconciliation with his daughter,
and afterward she'd suffered guilt over that sad fact for a
very long time.

Irene O'Day had focused her needs and wishes on
Jolie, and it had been difficult to live up to her mother's
expectations. If she disagreed or tried to assert her own
individuality about anything from clothing styles to the
boys she dated, her mother reacted with where-did-I-go-
wrong martyrdom. Early on Jolie had given up fighting
and had let her mother live through her.

Morgan stroked the hair away from Jolie's face when
she told him about Stephen. She'd known the Merediths
all her life and loved Stephen almost like a brother. Then
the O'Days moved, and the two didn't meet again until
their college days.

Not only did they have a lifetime of shared memories
between them, but they had a future of discoveries as
well. The actual courtship had been brief, because they
hadn't felt the need to get acquainted.

But the adult Stephen Meredith turned out to be far
different from the boy Jolie had admired. There was a
dark side to his nature, and it wasn't long after the wed-
ding before she became aware of it.

After he had a string of meaningless affairs, Jolie made
the difficult decision to seek a divorce. His parents, her
mother and even Stephen to some extent tried to convince her to give him another chance. What they didn't
understand—what she couldn't explain—was the simple
fact that she couldn't settle for the second-rate attention
she received from Stephen.

She wanted someone who would love only her, forgive
her faults, share his life with her. She wanted more than a
physical relationship. She wanted a commitment, love
and respect. She wanted to share her mind and her heart
as well as her body.

She discovered her pregnancy before the divorce was filed. She suffered through another bout of Stephen's irrational accusations and spent a miserable nine months with him in hopes that maybe . . . perhaps . . . the baby would help him grow up and accept his responsibilities.

But it hadn't worked out that way. Jolie couldn't bring herself to tell Morgan the rest of the story just now. Maybe later, when her trust in him was more secure, she would be able to relate just how much Stephen's denial of his child and his false accusations had hurt her. Someday she would tell him how devastated she'd been when the Merediths, whom she'd always felt close to, supported Stephen and turned their backs on her and Meggie.

Now after several years she found it sadly ironic that they had readily accepted the idea of her adultery, an idea that Stephen had planted and nurtured. All the time they'd steadfastly refused to believe that their son was guilty of that very thing.

Now she lay quietly in the security of Morgan's arms, unwilling to spoil the mood by voicing the resentment and bitterness she still felt toward Stephen and his parents. She worried that it might somehow diminish her in his eyes and she so wanted him to have a high opinion of her. She wanted him to care for her as she cared for him.

She would tell him the rest someday. But not now. Now she wanted to savor the keenly sensuous pleasure of lying in his arms. She finished her story by saying, "My mother often remarked about history repeating itself, that Stephen left me just as my father had left her. I began to think I couldn't make a man happy."

"You never have to worry about that again," Morgan said gently, now understanding why she had so little confidence, why she shied away from men, why she tried to deny her feelings and even her femininity: It was her way of coping. He rushed to reassure her that her staunchly held defenses could be lowered at last.

"You're the most beautiful woman I've ever known. Beautiful inside and out, a rare quality. And you make me deliriously happy."

"Really?"

"Really. I'm a one-woman man, Jolie, and as long as we have a commitment, you'll never need to doubt my loyalty."

"What about Monica?" she asked tentatively. She'd often wondered about the woman Morgan chose not to discuss.

He smiled and outlined her passion-swollen lips with his fingertip. "I'm glad you brought that up. I want to get this out in the open, once and for all. Monica Jenet is just a good friend and a colleague."

Jolie smiled nervously. "A friend like I'm a friend?"

"You didn't believe that friendship bit for a moment," he accused gently. "You knew the motive behind that ruse. I was afraid you wouldn't have me under any other condition."

"Silly man," she said with a smile.

Morgan rewarded her with another light kiss. "Monica teaches French at the university, and we sometimes have lunch and discuss our work, but if that's going to be a problem, I can stop lunching with her."

Jolie bit his ear. "As long as it's only lunch she's after." She was surprised at her own generosity, but felt she could trust this man with her fragile heart. He was being honest and open.

"It is," he said, kissing the tip of her nose. "She's been out to the Leap a few times," Morgan continued. "Because Georgia was working on her French recipe chapter.

"Who knows? If you hadn't come along, something might have developed between us, but I doubt it. I've already told Monica all about you. She thinks it's wonderful that I've finally found the right woman." His hand stroked her back lazily. "I've told her that I'm serious about you."

"Are you?" Jolie asked with wonder and delight. Her fingertips trailed over his chest and tripped through the mat of fine golden hair.

Morgan released a long tense breath and pulled her into his arms. "Yes. Since the first moment I saw you. You make me feel things I've never felt before." Raising himself onto his elbows above her, he gently cradled her face in his hands. "What about you, Jolie?"

She sighed contentedly. Tomorrow the doubts might return, but right now she couldn't agree more. "Oh, yes."

Morgan groaned and kissed her. He wanted to kiss away her past, all the unhappiness she'd ever known. He wanted to erase all her memories of her ex-husband, replacing them with memories of their own. His lips tingled where her tongue ran provocatively over his mouth, then sizzled with the erotic sensations she prompted. Had he really been alive before he met her?

"I'm afraid you aren't going to get much sleep tonight," he mumbled, nuzzling her ear.

Jolie wanted to tell him how important he was to her. She wanted to secure his promise to be patient while she learned to deal with her newly awakened emotions; they'd been dormant for so long. But Morgan was initiating another round of breathtaking pleasure and her mind could not form, much less voice, her thoughts.

"There are still several hours before dawn." She caught her breath as his hand roamed intimately over secret places.

"Not nearly enough," he said with a sigh.

CHAPTER NINE

Jolie awoke bathed in sunlight and glory.

The brightening daylight touched the still sleeping Morgan with gold, burnishing his hair and warming his skin. Jolie stroked his back gently, wonderingly. He stirred but buried his face deeper into the big pillow he clutched in his folded arms. It seemed so natural to wake up beside him, she thought as she trailed her fingertips down the long length of him.

Last night he'd called her his lady. But what did that mean?

No words of love had been spoken, no promises for the future were made. Did he mean she was his for now? For the moment? Or did his words mean something more? Jolie wondered how she should proceed. She had little experience in dealing with situations like this.

She didn't understand how he had become so important to her so quickly, but she knew as she lay in the love-rumpled bed with the rosy glow of morning washing over her that her life would never be the same again.

Now that she knew him, she wasn't at all sure she could ever be completely happy without hearing the ring of his laughter, without feeling the gentleness of his touch. How could she do without the security of his arms around her? It would be a pitiful existence without his whimsy and wit, without his easygoing ability to put things into perspective and his passion for drawing the joy from life.

She had never expected to find this kind of love, and now that she had discovered it with Morgan, she was frightened. Could it really happen like this or had he bewitched her with his tenderness, his charm? She shivered slightly when she realized that she had now passed the emotional point of no return.

Morgan drew one arm from under his pillow and draped it across her chest. It was a proprietary gesture, but he was feeling quite possessive this morning. Possessive and content. When he felt her body tremble beneath his arm, he ran his hand over her shoulder to see if her skin was cool. The action was so rewarding, he repeated the gesture and spoke without opening his eyes. "Do you need warming up, sweetheart?"

Morgan was so perfectly attuned to her, emotionally as well as physically, that he'd noticed the involuntary shivering of her body. Jolie also knew that she couldn't voice the thoughts tumbling about in her mind. She wouldn't think about tomorrow, for he was here now. He was hers now. "I think," she said, striving for a light tone, "that the residual heat from last night could keep me warm at the North Pole."

Morgan flipped over and smiled, stretching his rangy frame luxuriously and yawning expansively. He rolled on top of her, grabbing her playfully. "You know what I like even better than heating up the night?"

"No." Jolie had a good idea. The way he was caressing her breast was a clue she could hardly ignore. "Do tell."

"Nah, it'd take too long. I think I'll show you instead."

Later, Morgan held her close and kissed the top of her head. "You're a beautiful lover, Jolie, so soft and so sweet. You touch me in a way no other woman ever has."

"I don't think I really knew the meaning of making love until last night. I know it sounds silly—after all, I'm

123

divorced and have had a child—but it's almost as if it were the first time."

"That isn't silly, it's wonderful." He brushed back her hair and kissed her forehead. "I know, love, because I have the same silly, wonderful feeling."

They lay together in peaceful immobility for several long minutes. Too soon they would have to part and real life would intrude. Jolie had never been separated from Meggie for long and she was eager to find out how her daughter had fared on her first night away from home.

Morgan reached for his watch on the bedside table. "Uh-oh, we're going to have to move it."

"Move what?" Jolie was precariously close to falling asleep again despite her good intentions. She hadn't gotten much rest last night.

Morgan eased gently away from her and sat on the edge of the bed, watching her over his shoulder. God, she made it hard to get out of bed. He slapped her pretty little rump lightly. "Get up, sweetheart. Move it. We have big things to do today."

"Such as?" she mumbled.

"The house raising. Didn't I tell you about that?"

Jolie was awake now. She sat up, fighting the impulse to clutch the sheet modestly. She wouldn't be hiding anything he wasn't already intimately familiar with. "It must have slipped your mind. What house raising?"

"I've invited a bunch of people out to the Leap to help me finish Georgia's house. It won't be so much a raising as it will be a finishing. We still have to shingle the roof, plank the floors, put up the plaster board, paint and install the electrical fixtures." He headed for the bathroom. "Mind if I shower first?"

"Wait a minute. Let me get this straight. You're going to do all that today? Just how many people did you invite?"

Morgan shrugged, wishing she would pull up that damned sheet. Those perky breasts of hers might just be grounds for abandoning the entire project. "I lost track. But the men are bringing their wives, kids, food and beer and we're making a day of it. It'll be fun."

"When is this bit of Americana scheduled to take place?"

"Soon. Now get the lead out. It wouldn't do for the host and hostess to be late." Morgan turned on the shower and called over the din, "Why don't you invite your friend and her Viking? I'd like to get to know them better."

Before he stepped behind the gold-tinted shower door, he seriously considered dragging Jolie in with him. No, he decided, if he did that they'd never get out of the house. As the warm spray beat down on him, Morgan wondered at his good fortune. He'd always hoped to find a woman exactly like her but had begun to think his expectations were unrealistic. Last night had been proof that perfection was possible.

Fresh from his shower, his towel-dried hair still damp and smelling of Jolie's herbal shampoo, Morgan reluctantly agreed to go ahead without her. "You won't be too long, will you?"

Jolie drew her hand across her heart in a childhood gesture. "Cross my heart. I have to get ready and pick up Meggie. I can't show up looking like this."

Jolie was referring to her tousled hair and kiss-swollen lips, but Morgan swept his gaze over her naked form. "I'll say you can't. You'd start a riot such as Lady Godiva never saw."

She pulled on her silken robe and knotted the sash. At the front door he kissed her and headed for his car. He leaned his chin on his arms where they rested on the car's roof. "Hurry. I can't wait to show off my lady." Blowing her another kiss, he ducked inside.

His lady.

Jolie fairly skipped into the bedroom and flung her robe on the unmade bed. Why did Morgan's air of loving

125

possession thrill her so much? She pondered the question as she faced the stream of the shower. By the time she stepped onto the bath mat and wrapped a huge pink towel around herself, Jolie had reached a most satisfying conclusion.

With Morgan she was free to share as much of herself as she was ready to share. He hadn't pried into her past, hadn't asked the questions she knew he must have wanted answered. She was certain he would wait patiently until she told him the full story.

She was his lady, the one he chose to spend his time with, the one he chose to share his body and perhaps his heart with. But she was still in charge of her own life. Morgan believed she was capable of making her own decisions, and he respected her.

Stephen had been so insecure, he'd insisted on governing all her activities. She had never had a single thought that he didn't want to be privy to. When he'd returned from his frequent business trips, he'd expected a documentation of how she'd spent every moment, demanding to know where she had gone, whom she had seen. It was much later before she realized he was projecting his own indiscretions onto her.

While Stephen had demanded control of her life, he had chosen not to let her into his completely. Throughout their three-year marriage he'd managed to keep her at arm's length, never trusting her, never sharing any real intimacy. The handsome, athletic boy she'd known all her life became a stranger after their marriage.

It was years before she understood that the reason Stephen behaved as he did was that he had never admitted that she had grown up. To him, she would always be the shy, skinny little kid who had followed him around as a child and idolized him as an adolescent. He had never let her be a woman, and he had never become a man. Stephen had not respected or trusted her abilities.

The marriage was doomed to failure, but she had

126

fought for it . . . how she had fought for it. And at such cost.

In her relationship with Morgan, though it was still new, they were on equal footing. She sensed that with him there would be a give and take, an unfolding and enfolding, a meshing of two lives, by two people who chose that path together.

Would she share her life with Morgan? That possibility both frightened and elated her.

The late-morning air was clear and brisk, and everywhere sunlight buttered the landscape. Overhead frothy white clouds towed their shadows across the low green treetops. As Jolie drove to Morgan's, she began to think fancifully that the perfect day had been made just for her. And her perfect man as well.

She glanced at Meggie, buckled safely into the seat beside her. She had apparently had a wonderful time at Barbara's. Her daughter was full of all the things she and Ryan had done and seemed to boast a new self-confidence, a new sense of herself. Despite the guilt she felt at leaving the child overnight, Jolie was glad she had finally taken the first steps to loosening her rigid control over Meggie. They would both benefit.

Following Morgan's directions, she drove down a road that took her some distance past Morgan's house. At the building site the roadside was lined with cars. Finding the nearest slot, Jolie parked and helped Meggie out of the van. There was no sign of either Sharon's or Sven's car, and she assumed they hadn't yet arrived. She wanted her best friends to get to know Morgan and was glad they'd accepted the invitation.

Leading Meggie and balancing the two pecan pies she'd picked up to contribute to the communal feast, Jolie scanned the yard, hoping for a glimpse of Morgan.

He called her name, and she looked up to find him straddling the roof of his mother's new home. He was bare to the waist, and his muscles rippled under the gleaming coat of perspiration he'd worked up. He wore low-slung blue jeans with a carpenter's apron knotted around his slim waist. He grinned and waved a hammer in greeting.

Jolie waved back and watched him hand his tools to another worker before climbing down the ladder. He crossed the lawn in long strides, stopping only long enough to douse his head with a garden hose. He swung his head in a great arc, and the water droplets glistened, spraying in every direction.

Her heart overflowed with love for him and Jolie feared it might burst at the sight of him.

"Hi, love," he said before kissing her quickly but thoroughly. "I missed you. What took you so long?"

"It's only been two hours since I last saw you," she gently admonished.

"Funny, it seemed longer." He scooped Meggie into his arms, planting a tickling kiss on her cheek. "I'm glad to see you, too." He cared almost as much for the little girl as he did for her mother and held her tightly for a moment before allowing her to squirm free.

"Where Tess. Where bunnies. Where kitties."

Morgan grimaced, and Jolie laughed. "I guess you can see where you rate on her hit parade."

"I'm not above stooping to a little gentle bribery if it wins points," he allowed.

"Mommy look. Aunt Shar. Fen." Meggie took off across the lawn to greet the new arrivals. Then they approached, each holding one of Meggie's hands.

Jolie had the distinct feeling that she must look as well loved as she felt, because Sharon shot her a thumbs-up gesture of a job well done behind Morgan's back.

Then Sven indicated his interest in the project. "I am happy to assist in your American house rearing. It will be something to write my family about."

"House *raising*, Sven darling," Sharon corrected.

128

"Raising, rearing." He shrugged. "The house goes up."

"It sure does." Morgan laughed. "Let me put Sven to work and I'll be back to introduce you ladies around. Put your food wherever you can find an empty spot." He and Sven turned toward the cottage, their blond heads bent together in conversation.

"Look at them. God, how did we get so lucky?" Sharon sighed dreamily.

"Pure living, no doubt," Jolie deadpanned.

"So what's my excuse?" Sharon was always joking at her own expense.

Tables had been set up in the shade of some old oak trees near the new house. They were covered with quaint red-and-white-checked cloths and food of every imaginable description. Women fussed around the tables, trying to keep their children's little fingers out of the tempting array of dishes.

Meggie was soon playing happily with the other children, who ranged in every size from infants to teens. Jolie wondered how a bachelor like Morgan came to have so many families as friends. It took only a moment to realize that he just liked people, old, young, big or little. And apparently everybody liked him. People certainly turned out in force when he asked for their help.

Sharon waved coyly in the direction of the cottage, where the noise of ringing hammers and buzzing saws added to the sounds of playing children and laughing adults. "I'll see you later. I think I'll just mosey on over and watch Sven's muscles ripple."

Jolie glanced around and found Meggie under a tree with another little girl about her size. Both were cuddling flop-eared rabbits on their laps. She wandered around the lawn, speaking to the women she'd met earlier and dodging the scampering children. She spotted Tess munching on some blood-red tulips and wondered if the bulbs had been planted solely for the equine's dining pleasure.

The grounds around the cottage site as well as those at

129

the Leap were verdant, with wildflowers blooming profusely among the tulips and naturalized daffodils. Star-of-Bethlehem buttoned up the grassy expanse of the lawn, their tiny flowers gleaming pure white in the sunlight. Although the landscaping was new, it was lush and beautiful, but not nearly as vibrant as the area surrounding Morgan's home.

He had created a safe, restful haven. It would be a wonderful place for her and Meggie to live.

No sooner had her mind formed the thought than she called it back. Was she already thinking of the future? Morgan had made no promises concerning that. He had told her she was his lady, but he hadn't mentioned Meggie. How did her daughter fit into his scheme of things?

She stopped to watch a group of youngsters wading in the little stream, and although she couldn't see the Leap from this distance, she knew that it was the same stream that crossed in front of Morgan's house. How had he managed to construct his home without disturbing the natural beauty of the creek?

There was so much she wanted to know about the man she had come to love. Why had he built such a fairy-tale house? What did he think about when he stood in the tower on a starry night? What stroke of luck, what magic had brought this enchanting man to Norman, Oklahoma, and into her heart?

"Watch out for frogs," warned a delightfully familiar voice from behind her. Morgan slipped his arms around her waist and hugged her close to his bare chest. The heat she felt radiating from him might have come from exertion, but Jolie preferred to think it had not.

"And 'horny' toads?" Jolie teased.

They laughed together as she leaned into his strength and asked two of her many questions. "Isn't this the same stream that flows in front of the Leap? How did you manage to build your home without ruining it?"

"Yes. Most people don't realize it's the same one."

130

Morgan nuzzled her neck before he said, "It was a marvel of engineering and hard work. I couldn't get any equipment close to the building site and I had to lug rocks that had been piled on the driveway." Morgan's right hand caressed her hip, causing Jolie's lung capacity to deteriorate.

"Quit fooling around, Morgan," she reproved in a husky tone of voice that had the ability to make him go weak in the knees. "I get sidetracked when you do that."

"If we talk now can we fool around later?" he whispered into her hair.

Jolie was ready to fool around with Morgan for the rest of her life. "I'd be disappointed if we didn't."

"I'd never knowingly disappoint you, love." Morgan tightened the circle of his arms under her breasts. "I didn't want to kill the ferns or flowers with truck tires. And I had to be extra careful with the mortar so as not to spoil the stream with any debris."

And whether you know it or not, he added silently, it was all for you, Jolie. Throughout the construction of the house, he'd had a vague image of the woman he wanted to share it with. Jolie was that woman.

"Why?"

"Why, what?" He wished they were at the Leap at this very moment. He had an overwhelming urge to scoop her up into his arms and . . .

"Why did you build it yourself, stone by stone, board by board? You could have hired a crew to build it and they'd have been out of there in a few months instead of years."

"It wouldn't have been the same," he said thoughtfully. "I guess it was something I wanted to do myself. I wanted to develop a sense of oneness with the place, a sense of belonging. That's why I built my house around the stream, the trees. I could have had the land razed and then landscaped after the construction, but I wanted the house to be part of the land, not vice versa."

131

He laughed self-consciously. "I guess that all sounds a bit sappy, doesn't it."

"Not at all," Jolie said, caressing his arms with her hands. She was moved by the sensitivity of this strong man.

"The first time I saw the area where I decided to build, it was little more than a clearing in the woods. But I walked around it and I felt something that's hard to explain. I felt as though there were benevolent spirits there or something. It may sound silly, but something drew me there and told me that I was home."

"I know." Jolie understood his feelings completely because she had experienced some of the same feelings about the Leap, as though it was special. But not nearly as special as this man.

"Before you think me a paragon of virtue, let me explain that I had help with the inside, just as we have help today finishing Georgia's cottage. It's not completely the house that Morgan built."

"To me it is." Smiling, Jolie tried to imagine him tiptoeing over wildflowers and toadstools, being careful not to disturb the spirits that inhabited the place. The more she discovered about him, the more she loved him.

The late-afternoon picnic lunch evolved into a marathon eating session when Jolie attempted to sample each of the appetizing dishes. Morgan teased her about the hefty size of her laden plate, but she assured him it was all in the interest of her business. She was always on the prowl for tempting new dishes to introduce at the restaurant.

Finally, declaring she could eat no more, she collapsed under a spreading oak tree, where she was promptly joined by Morgan. Meggie played nearby with another new friend and a couple of the barn cat's kittens.

Morgan stretched out beside her and put his head in her lap. "Think you'll ever want to eat again?" he asked lazily.

"Not for a few hours at least." Jolie stroked his forehead, smoothing back the lively blond hair. She felt replete, not only from the food but from sharing the day with Morgan. She was drowsy from overeating and might have fallen asleep if Georgia hadn't chosen that moment to approach them.

"Mind if I join you?" she asked as she gingerly lowered herself to the ground.

Morgan opened one eye and squinted it against the dappled sunlight. "Make yourself comfortable," he said wryly. "It's your blade of grass now."

"I don't think I've had a chance to congratulate you on your new book, Mrs. Asher," Jolie said.

"Thanks, Jolie, but for cripe's sake call me Georgia!"

Jolie watched Morgan's lips curve into a smile but he didn't say a word. "Tell me about your trip to New York, Georgia. From what Morgan tells me, it sounds exciting."

"It's something my agent cooked up. When you're a celebrity you've gotta make yourself available to your public. I'll be signing books in eleven cities and doing local talk shows. Barnaby is going with me this time, so it won't be all work and no play." She cackled with laughter and jabbed Jolie lightly in the ribs.

"You are a devil," Morgan accused. "You really should try to tone down in your old age."

"Well, when my old age gets here, I might just do that." Georgia cackled again, then turned on her son. "And don't you be so fresh, young man! You ought to be ashamed to talk to your mother like that. Besides, I'm not that damned old."

"Of course you're not." Morgan smiled again. It was a great feeling to be surrounded by his three favorite females—he felt like the indolent master of a lion pride.

"The cottage is looking good." Georgia stared out to the new construction, where a few ambitious types were still hard at work. "Nevada's in a snit today and refused to come. She claimed she had an upset stomach, so I made her some chicken soup. Caught her feeding it to that damned hound of hers. That woman is going to drive me to drink."

"It's your own fault you have to put up with her. I told you that you're welcome to stay with me at the Leap. By the way," he added teasingly, "when did you give up drinking?"

"With the child I managed to be stuck with, it seems I'd have been better off to give up something else," the older woman complained. "Besides, I don't want to cramp your style and I sure as hell don't need you around to cramp mine. It's already taken you too damn long to find a wife as it is. I swear, Morgan—"

"Yes," he agreed with a laugh. "Like a sailor."

Jolie and Morgan exchanged knowing looks regarding Georgia's comment about cramping styles. It was just as Morgan had said—Georgia was a very independent woman.

Georgia rolled her eyes toward the heavens. "What did I ever do?" she wailed. Then she smiled at Jolie. "He's a damn brat, Jolie, and don't ever say that I didn't warn you."

"I'll keep that in mind, Georgia." Jolie grinned down at the brat just in time to catch his sassy wink.

"As I was about to say, Morgan," Georgia reminded him, "do you think the house will be ready for me to move in when I get back?"

"Should be."

"No thanks to you," she said, admonishing her son as if he were a recalcitrant ten-year-old. "Why aren't you out there helping your friends, young man? Do you expect them to do all the work?"

"No, ma'am. I was just letting my lunch settle first. Have you forgotten your old rule about waiting at least an hour?"

"That's before swimming, you idiot. I don't think

you're in danger of developing stomach cramps while wielding a paintbrush."

Jolie laughed at the good-natured bickering between mother and son. It made her miss her own mother, although their relationship had never been as easy as the Ashers'. Irene O'Day had never been the independent woman Georgia appeared to be.

Jolie's mother had always been timid and fearful, afraid of being alone, afraid of asserting herself. After Jolie's father left, she'd grown worse. He had left them well provided for, but in doing so had made sure that Irene never had to make her own way. She had lived only for and through her daughter, and Jolie had found the burden almost too much to bear.

When Jolie decided to leave Stephen, Irene had insisted that Jolie move in with her. That had not been Jolie's plan, but upon learning of her mother's illness, she'd returned to her childhood home—and to her childhood self. It had been a struggle to be both Meggie's mother and Irene's daughter.

"Just try to have it ready for me when I get back," Georgia said, interrupting Jolie's thoughts. "Three weeks should be long enough to furnish it and put out the welcome mat."

"You should choose your own furniture, Georgia," he insisted.

"You know I don't give a fig for decorating. I live to cook and to write about it. As long as it's comfortable and reasonably attractive, I'll take whatever I get. Never could resist a grab bag."

"Your home should wear your personal stamp, Georgia," Jolie said in an attempt to help Morgan out. "It should be as individual as your wardrobe."

Georgia tossed back her mop of curls and howled. "Damn, I wouldn't want it to look as individual as *my* wardrobe." She smoothed out the leg of her lime green jumpsuit, whose pockets were huge red appliquéd apples, both inhabited by fat-cheeked green worms.

"She's right, Jolie. We'd better do it."

"Just scrounge some of that junk you've got stashed in that monstrosity of yours. A piece here, a piece there. Hell, you'll never even miss it."

"Why don't I just hang around at the different charity drop boxes? It'll save you a lot of money. And with your taste, I doubt if you'd notice the difference anyway."

"You should have been drowned as a pup, Morgan. How in hell did you get so ornery? Are you gonna do it or not?"

"Don't worry, Georgia," Jolie promised. "I'll make sure your new home is ready and waiting for you when you get back." She grinned at Morgan. "If it's all right with you, of course."

"You know, Jolie," Georgia said before her son could reply, "I'm glad this boy of mine finally found a level-headed young woman like you. I know you'll be a good stabilizing influence on him. Heaven knows, I've tried but I just can't figure out where he gets his outrageous personality. His dear daddy was a saint."

She stared thoughtfully into the distance. "I did have a crazy cousin, though. But we always thought it was the drink that ruined him." Georgia tossed her head dismissively. "Oh well, I'm glad Morgan showed enough sense to pick someone like you. I guess he realized by now that there's only room in the clock for one cuckoo."

Morgan jumped nimbly to his feet and pulled his diminutive mother into his arms, giving her a bear hug until she squirmed in protest. "That's why we're building you a nest of your own, love."

By late afternoon the work had stopped; the cottage was finished. Georgia presided over a ceremonial lighting of lights, with her guests crowded into the small house. She gave the result of their enterprise her unqualified approval, and a boisterous cheer went up.

Morgan thanked all his friends for their unstinting efforts and proclaimed, "Let the merrymaking begin!"

Instruments were brought out and a regular hoedown ensued.

Jolie enjoyed several dances with Morgan; however, she had a difficult time keeping up with the fast steps of the Western line dance. She clapped in time with the pounding rhythms while Morgan swirled with Meggie clutched in his arms. The child was weak with giggles when he put her back on her feet. She waved to her mother briefly before running off to find her new friends.

Morgan squeezed Jolie's hand. "Let's slip away for a little while. I want to show you something special."

"What about Meggie? I can't just go off and leave her alone."

"Alone?" He grinned. "There must be seventy-five people here. She couldn't be alone if she wanted to be."

"But no one else knows to watch her the way I do," Jolie stalled. "She isn't used to being unsupervised."

"Then it's time she was. If it'll make you feel better, we'll find Georgia and—look. They're way ahead of us."

Jolie smiled at the picture of Meggie and Morgan's tiny mother stomping through a vigorous square dance.

"I think my mother has adopted Meggie as the grandchild she despaired of ever having."

"Looks like Meggie has adopted her as the grandmother she's never known."

Morgan looked at her intently. It had been his impression that Meggie's paternal grandparents were alive. "But she does have grandparents. Doesn't she?"

"My mother died when Meggie was an infant and my father passed on several years before that."

"What about the Merediths?"

"Stephen's parents chose not to be part of Meggie's life, just as he did."

Morgan didn't know what to say. He couldn't understand people denying the familial bond between them and

137

their own flesh and blood. "But Meggie is their son's child," he said, astonished.

"Meggie is *my* daughter," Jolie said firmly. "Stephen convinced his parents that Meggie wasn't his child. He accused me of some pretty terrible things, and they believed him."

Morgan reeled at her words. He'd had no idea of the agonies she'd been through. "But there are tests, ways to prove . . ."

Jolie looked into his eyes unwaveringly. "Do you really think I would dignify his accusations by making my child undergo tests to prove her paternity? Stephen was the first and only man I'd ever been with until I met you. He just couldn't accept Meggie's handicap. He claimed she couldn't be his because she failed to live up to his expectations. He merely made up his mind that she had to be someone else's mistake."

Her voice quivered, emotion thickening her words. Morgan put his arm around her and drew her out of the knot of people. "Let it out, Jolie."

She took a deep breath. "When I realized I was pregnant, Stephen accused me of using it to trap him and his wealth. He only stayed with me until Meggie was born, because his parents threatened to cut off his funds if he didn't. I'm not sure if they entirely believed the things he said about me; they'd known me since I was a child."

Jolie wasn't sure she could go on. She wasn't sure she wanted to bare that painful part of her life to Morgan, but when he wrapped his arms around her, comforting and soothing her, she continued.

"Stephen had already informed me after two years of marriage that he didn't think he wanted children after all. After Meggie's birth and the subsequent discovery of her deafness, he let me know that a 'damaged' child wouldn't do."

Anger and helplessness tore through Morgan: anger at the man who'd made Jolie and Meggie suffer, and a crippling helplessness because there wasn't a damn thing he could do about it.

"You've probably noticed how much Meggie resembles me. Stephen used that in his plot to deny her. He was tall and blond like you, and I think eventually the Merediths began to believe him. They wanted to believe him."

"What happened?"

"They offered to settle a healthy sum on me, to buy me off. But I took my baby and moved in with my mother, who was terminally ill. I nursed her until the end and then I took my inheritance and moved here.

"I settled in Norman because of fond memories of my college days here. I bought the duplex and got reacquainted with Sharon, who was interested in opening a tearoom. We joined forces, and the rest you already know."

Morgan held her tightly for several minutes. He'd guessed that she'd known sorrow in her life but never had he imagined the depth of her pain. It was no wonder she didn't have any laugh lines. He felt fiercely protective of her and comforted himself somewhat with the knowledge that from now on anyone who threatened her happiness would have to go through him first.

"Come on, Jolie, you're coming with me." He caught his mother's attention, and she nodded once in understanding. "Georgia will watch Meggie while you and I relax a little. Are you willing?"

Jolie was past willing. She'd never felt so loved or protected in her entire life. She didn't have to think twice. "Yes," she answered somewhat breathlessly. "I'm willing."

He led her around the cottage and far down an overgrown path to what appeared to be an equipment shed.

"What are you doing?" she asked when he began feeling around the eaves of the building.

Morgan treated her to one of his rakish grins when he triumphantly pulled out a key and held it up for her inspection. "We're going to take a little ride. Ever ride a three-wheeler?"

"Yes," she answered smugly, feeling a delicious sense of freedom from her earlier unburdening. "But I gave it up for a bike with training wheels. Tricycles are for babies, you know."

Morgan chuckled as he swung open the door. The vehicle in question was a huge, expensive toy designed for men who'd never lost their youthful zest for life. Men like Morgan. The ATV was red, with two large balloon tires at the back, a small motor between them and a handlebar not unlike that of a motorcycle mounted over a smaller tire in the front. The seat was big enough for two.

"Get ready for the ride of your life, lady."

"Are we really going to ride on that?" she asked incredulously.

"Of course." Morgan stepped onto the bike, threw his leg over and straddled the monster in one deft move. He started the engine and scooted up to make room for her behind him.

"Where are we going?" she called as she climbed aboard.

Morgan turned quickly and placed a kiss on the tip of her upturned nose. "Don't be so inquisitive, love. Surely you recall what curiosity did to the cat?"

She laughed uninhibitedly as they sped over the countryside, up hill and down. Bouncing along behind him with the evening breeze blowing in her hair, Jolie felt as free as a bird. She was so happy to be right where she belonged: with Morgan.

The fact that she was racing through the twilight on a giant toy with no idea of where she might be headed didn't bother her at all.

CHAPTER TEN

Before long they neared Morgan's house and parked the bike. On foot they followed a path into the woods. At the end of it Morgan drew aside a hanging curtain of vines and pushed open a wooden gate, holding it for Jolie.

"Care to step into my boudoir?" Morgan asked with a come-hither gesture.

"Said the spider to the fly?" Jolie's brows knit in confusion. She'd expected them to go inside when they'd arrived at Morgan's house, but instead he'd brought her here. She stepped through the gate and was immediately glad they had come instead to this beautiful outdoor room. She couldn't believe something so tranquil could exist amid the tangled undergrowth of the woods, and she knew it had been created with a tender, loving hand.

"Oh, Morgan, it's beautiful. However did you manage it?"

More than pleased by her reaction, he grinned. "No engineering genius required here. Just plain old elbow grease."

Jolie walked around admiring the little glade. It had obviously been constructed, carved out of the blackjack and scrub oak that surrounded it. Yet it seemed totally natural. It was a place for elves and wee people to dance their fairy rings on a moonlit night.

In the early-evening shadows a weathered gray wooden fence was barely visible beneath a sprawl of honeysuckle and silverlace vines. The interior was roughly twenty-five by thirty-five feet, and the grass was as smooth and unmarred as a green carpet. Four stately maples marked the corners, and beneath their canopy bloomed a profusion of shade-loving flowers.

Only the center of the rectangle was open to the sun, and an ancient sundial stood there in regal dignity. Wild roses rambled over trellises, and Jolie could imagine the heady fragrance when summer brought their clustered blooms.

Morgan led her to a stone bench and they sat in the gathering gloom of twilight. The trees weren't yet in full leaf, but later in the season the place would be a cool haven from the merciless Oklahoma sun.

"Do you like it?" Suddenly her answer was of the utmost importance. He needed something from her, some sort of signal to let him know that he'd been right to bring her here to his special place. If it were in his power, he'd put all Jolie's unhappy memories in a bottle and cast it into the sea.

"*Like* is a tepid word for what I feel," Jolie admitted.

"Tell me what you feel."

"I feel at peace here. As if I'd be able to solve the problems of the universe if I could just sit here long enough. It feels like the rest of the world has dissolved and you and I are the only souls left."

"That's it. That's what I wanted to hear. You understand how it is with me. I wanted this place to be just as special for you as it is for me."

"It's unbelievable that in such wild disorder a thing of beauty can exist."

Morgan held her hands warmly in his. "It's like you, Jolie. Despite all the tangled problems and worries of your life, you exist whole and beautiful. You have to fight the dark things in life, like the weeds that could reclaim this place in a wink if I weren't vigilant.

"But we have to be careful, because sometimes in our

zeal to be rid of the weeds, we destroy the flowers as well." Morgan felt his chest tighten with emotion. It was important that she understand the meaning behind his words.

"Don't lock the good things out of your heart, Jolie, just because you fear the bad. That first night in your backyard you accused me of offering you Band-Aids. Maybe I was, but I didn't know what kind of wound I was dealing with. The first step to healing any hurt is to cleanse it. At least let me help you cleanse yourself of the past."

Jolie knew he was right. She'd never really allowed the pain of Stephen's rejection to heal. She'd kept it alive and festering with her bitterness. She slipped into Morgan's arms and kissed him with an urgency that was still new to her, still surprising to her.

He melded his mouth to hers. Even during their long night of lovemaking his kisses hadn't been so fierce. But now his lips asked no questions, offered no promises. Now they made demands, and Jolie's breath was nearly stolen away by the intensity he communicated to her.

His hands pressed against her back and burned against the skin above her sundress. Then they were in her hair, pulling her to him. Her arm slipped around his neck as she met each demand, giving as much as she got.

It seemed to her that the world had gone silent. The chirping and whirring of unseen birds and insects was drowned out by the blood pounding through her veins. Reluctantly she drew away, afraid she would expire from lack of oxygen.

"Morgan," she murmured. "Oh, Morgan, I love you so much." She had to say the words. She wasn't afraid her love wouldn't be returned—he'd already confirmed his feelings for her. She felt it in his straining body, in his searching hands, in his questing mouth. His actions asked the questions. Her words were the answer.

"Jolie, you don't know how long I've waited to find

143

you." He cradled her head against his chest, and her cheek brushed the gold-tipped hairs growing there. "I used the money my father left me to build the Leap, knowing I had to have this place from the first time I saw it. I knew I had to build my own little castle for the woman who would make it my home. I knew that you were that woman from the first moment I saw you. I knew I had to have you, too. I never want to lose you."

Jolie was shaken by his words. Morgan's declaration of love was just as passionate as everything else about him. It would be difficult to live up to the dreams of a lifetime. Could the real Jolie become Morgan's fantasy woman in the tower?

He kissed her again, and her doubts drifted away on the spring breeze.

Within the walls of the secret garden, they undressed each other slowly, lingering over the ritual to heighten their excitement. The cooling air made Jolie's skin tingle, and Morgan's feather-light touch aroused her cell by cell. By the time he laid her down in the sweet, dew-damp grass, every fiber of her being cried for relief.

His own trembling flesh answered her need and the fantasy blossomed into reality. They soon achieved a strange, wondrous rhythm, and the wantonness of her own body overwhelmed her.

Jolie squeezed her eyes shut, trapped in a swirling red haze as deep and shimmering as the sensations burning inside her. The last delicious moments came on them simultaneously and a sudden release of abundant happiness engulfed them, threatening to overpower them with its intensity.

They lay side by side in the slow-cooling aftermath, a rich green carpet of grass beneath them, a few early stars overhead. The pungent fragrance of the earth filled Jolie's nostrils and the amplified sounds of nature filled her ears. Morgan Asher filled her body and her heart with a joy she had thought impossible to attain.

There were no words to express her feelings, yet never had two people communicated so much in silence. They shared a beautiful, age-old secret.

Morgan enjoyed the blush that colored Jolie's cheeks as she dressed and flicked grass out of her hair. Was this shy creature the same one who had just loved him with such passionate abandon? Love for her sang through his veins.

"Why did you go to all the trouble of building this garden, Morgan? It must have taken many hours of hard work to clear this place."

"It wasn't so bad. A man needs something to keep him out of trouble, and hacking out underbrush is as good as anything."

Jolie should have expected him to make light of his accomplishment. "But why did you create it?"

"You're a big one for the why of things, aren't you?" he said as he got to his feet and extended his hand to pull her up. "I just wanted a retreat from life, where I could sit and vegetate and ponder. I like to watch the squirrels and birds at play. I hope someday I can watch our children playing here also."

Jolie blinked and swallowed. "Our children?"

The alarm in her voice surprised him. "We can't let Meggie be an only child. I want to adopt her after we're married, then later give her some little brothers and sisters."

"After we're married?"

"I never realized that this place had an echo before." Morgan laughed, pulling her into his arms. "Yes. After we're married. Which, with any luck, won't be too far in the future."

Jolie felt a trickle of panic. It was one thing to admit her love, quite another to commit herself to a second marriage. And other children. She had been wondering about Morgan not offering any plans for the future. Well, he was offering them now.

"I wasn't aware that you wanted to adopt Meggie," she said slowly.

"Of course I do. I love that little kid as much as I love her mother. I want her to belong to both of us."

"Morgan, I don't think I want other children. I'm not sure that I have enough love to offer another child. Meggie is just too important to me, too much part of my life."

"I know she is. But love isn't some finite thing you have to divide and ration. Even if we have half a dozen children, you'll find you have more than enough love to go around."

They walked back to the three-wheeler and Jolie tried to quell her growing sense of resentment. How could she resent Morgan and the love he offered her? He wanted to be Meggie's father, her husband.

She'd thought she was ready to let go of the past and embrace a future filled with happiness. But as they bounced over the bumps and ruts back to the cottage site, Jolie was no longer so sure. She wasn't sure she could let anyone, even Morgan, into the insulated world she had built for Meggie and herself. Why did things always have to be so complicated? she wondered as Morgan relocked the shed.

Jolie knew something was wrong when she saw the cluster of people under the oak tree. The sun was going down and it was hard to tell what was going on, but her finely honed instincts told her Meggie was involved.

"Oh my God! Meggie!" she cried when she saw her limp daughter cradled in Georgia's thin arms. She pushed through the knot of people and fell to her knees beside them. Fear struck her in the chest like a padded fist when she saw the trickle of blood on Meggie's forehead.

"Now, now, Jolie. Calm down," Georgia crooned. "She's going to be all right. Just got the wind knocked out of her. I've already checked and nothing's broken." Georgia gave up possession of the child to her mother.

146

"But she's bleeding. Look." Jolie stared at the drying red stain on Meggie's forehead. "I think I should get her to the hospital."

"I don't think there's any need for that. It's just a tiny cut at her hairline," Georgia pointed out calmly and reasonably. "It's already stopped bleeding and you can hardly tell where the skin is broken."

"What happened?" Morgan asked, hovering over Jolie and Meggie.

Barnaby, who appeared to be the only one in a dither, tried to explain. "Little Meggie's kitten climbed up the tree and couldn't get down. At least that's what the other children told us. She went up after it and slipped and fell. But, Jolie," he said in a reassuring voice, "she didn't fall very far. Why, a little mite like her couldn't have climbed very high."

Meggie stirred and blinked her wide brown eyes. "Hi Mommy. Where kitty. Kitty high, Meggie fall."

"I know, sweetie. You'll be all right in a few minutes." Relief and guilt and a hundred other emotions thundered through Jolie like a herd of runaway horses. How could she have been so selfish as to just go off into the woods with Morgan like that? Every time she left Meggie alone, something happened. She just couldn't take it anymore. She couldn't stand the feeling that she was somehow letting Meggie down.

While she'd been with Morgan, lost in a world of sensuous pleasure, her child had been hurt.

Morgan saw the look Jolie sent him and he read her thoughts. She was blaming herself for Meggie's accident. She was blaming him and the time they'd spent together. He could feel the chill of her accusations even though none had been voiced. She seemed to be miles away, though only inches separated them.

He carried Meggie inside the cottage, much to her protest at leaving the other children and the animals. She really wasn't hurt, and for that he was grateful. For a

147

moment, when he'd seen her lying so still and pale in Georgia's arms, he'd felt terrible panic.

They soon had Meggie cleaned up and she was her old self again, hurrying outdoors to rejoin her new playmates. Jolie, however, was noticeably different. She was quiet, and her very silence was damning.

Morgan followed behind her as she gathered Meggie's belongings in preparation to go home. "Jolie, about what happened—"

"Don't, Morgan. I can't talk about it now. I just want to get her home. I need some time to think about everything that's happened. I need time to understand how I feel."

"Talk to me, Jolie. Tell me how you feel." Morgan didn't want her to leave like this. There was too much uncertainty between them.

"I feel cheap and unwholesome and selfish," she whispered fiercely. Wheeling away from the hand that would comfort her, she spit out, "If anything had happened to Meggie while I was—was—with you, I never would have forgiven myself."

"Or me?"

"Or you."

"Jolie, please, Meggie wasn't hurt. Look at her. She's already forgotten the whole incident. From the first time I met you, you've been telling me that you don't like people to make a big deal out of her deafness, because you don't want her to be treated differently from other children."

"That's right. I don't," Jolie insisted.

"Well, wake up. Did you notice how she fit into the group of children here today? Did you notice how well she communicates with everyone when she's left to her own devices? Georgia, Barnaby—everyone adores her. She's bright, beautiful and endears herself to everyone she meets. The only handicap she has to live with is a mother who won't allow her to be normal."

148

Jolie looked as if he'd slapped her. Her eyes widened, swimming with tears, and Morgan had to be strong to face the pain and censure he saw there.

"How dare you?"

"I dare because I love you. I love you both." He grabbed her by the shoulders and shook her slightly. "Look, Jolie, I know you want to protect Meggie. Every parent wants to protect her child from the bad things in life. But is climbing up a tree to get a kitten such a terrible thing? Is getting the breath knocked out of her and a bump on the head such a fearsome event? Jolie, it wouldn't be *normal* for her to get through childhood without those things. She's a kid, dammit, not some hothouse flower who's going to perish in the bright light of day."

Jolie felt the air go out of her lungs and she slumped against him. Everything Morgan said was true. She was just as guilty of smothering her child with love as her own mother had been. Meggie could live with her physical handicap. Did she really want to burden her with an emotional one as well?

She buried her face against Morgan's hard chest and felt reassured by the steady thumping of his heart. "Be patient with me, Morgan. Everything has happened so fast that I feel a little confused. I know fairy tales are supposed to be like this, but I prefer to deal in reality. Help me make us a reality."

He didn't speak, couldn't speak, but he applied the gentle pressure of his lips to hers, telling her without words of his agreement. The quiet strength of his arms and the warmth of his mouth on hers told Jolie that he was ready to meet that challenge.

During the days that followed Jolie and Morgan found time to be together despite their busy schedules and the demands of their careers. With daylight saving time came

149

more hours of sunlight, and they spent the evenings furnishing Georgia's cottage.

Along with larger pieces they purchased for Georgia, Jolie and Morgan dragged a few choice items of furniture from the attic of the big house and scavenged pieces from Morgan's collections to create a picture-book perfection in the smaller house. They toted boxes of Georgia's belongings from the garage where they'd been stored and put away her dishes, antique cooking utensils, pottery and books.

Soon the house was ready to receive its new tenant.

With Meggie's enthusiastic help they planted brown-eyed susans, rose-of-sharon bushes, yarrow and lilac in a quaint dooryard garden reminiscent of the English countryside. They designed an herb garden, and Morgan cleared the land and laid the low stone retaining wall. A garden spot tilled and ready to plant would be the best surprise of all for Georgia, and Jolie was touched by Morgan's thoughtfulness.

When the kittens were ready to be weaned, Morgan gave Meggie her pick. She chose a fat little calico with wide amber eyes. The wad of fur was promptly named Daisy and became the child's affectionate sidekick, toted about as uncomplainingly as a toy.

Jolie made an effort to give Meggie more freedom, and before long she was wandering around Morgan's country place at will. With his help, she learned proper tree climbing techniques, and although Jolie's heart was frequently in her throat at her daughter's antics, she silently cheered the progress made by them both.

Morgan settled comfortably into the place he'd carved for himself in both Jolie's and Meggie's affections. Their relationship was one of shared intimacy and laughter. He knew Jolie was still troubled by uncertainty at times, but he was sure that both time and love would conquer the last of her doubts. Before long he began to mark time as "before Jolie" and "after Jolie."

Since the incident the day of the house raising, Jolie had been reluctant to leave Meggie in anyone else's care overnight. Morgan respected her wishes but longed for more time to spend alone with her, time to bring to fruition all the erotic thoughts and daydreams that plagued him.

That was why he was surprised when on the last weekend before Georgia's scheduled return, Jolie informed him she had arranged for Meggie to spend Saturday night with Sharon. Not one to look a gift horse in the mouth, Morgan asked no questions and quickly made plans to ensure that their time together would be memorable.

Jolie vetoed his suggestion that they get away to a resort by reminding him that she had never spent the night at the Leap. "I'm dying to get you naked in that scandalous bed of yours," she told him. That was the sort of demise he would be willing to risk.

On Saturday afternoon Jolie and Morgan fed his menagerie and she dusted her palms on the side of her jeans. "Now what about me? I'm ravenous."

Morgan pulled her into his arms. "Me too. Ever make love in a barn? In the hay?"

"Not in this life. But I've been developing my sense of adventure ever since I met you."

Morgan drew a shuddering breath and rested his fingertips lightly on her cheek. Their eyes met in a timeless gaze that made Jolie forget all about her hunger for food. She knew only a deep physical craving for one man as he brushed his lips across hers, then intensified the kiss into the sweetest agony she'd ever experienced.

Her hands slid up the front of his knit shirt, and his tongue flickered against hers. A roaring filled his ears, a dizziness spiraled his senses and a familiar ache of desire prompted him to carry her to a freshly pitched pile of hay to enhance her sense of adventure even more.

Later he wrapped his arm around her shoulders as

151

they strolled to the house. Jolie's arm quickly found its way to his waist and she hugged him.

"I'm still hungry, Morgan," she said.

"You're insatiable," he said.

Jolie grinned mischievously. "Maybe so, but I'm hungry too."

Chuckling, he escorted her into the kitchen. "Okay, you make the sandwiches and bring them up to my room."

"And what will you be doing?" Jolie nudged him with her elbow to indicate she hadn't missed his chauvinistic order.

"I'm going to fill that monstrous bathtub to the brim with bubbles for you. Sound good?" Morgan reached out and plucked a straw from her hair.

"Mmmm. Sounds wonderful. Just the thing after a tumble in the hay." She sighed as he left the room. He knew all the right moves, she thought.

She delighted in his thoughtfulness, his gentleness, his craziness. She loved everything about him. The better she came to know him, the more she loved him. What had happened to all those old insecurities that had plagued her for so long? She had been treated to a miraculous cure, and Morgan Asher was the miracle worker.

In the refrigerator Jolie found three kinds of cheese, a bunch of grapes, thick slices of ham and a bottle of wine. She rummaged through the cabinets and drawers until she found crackers, wineglasses and knives. They didn't need a feast, she reasoned, just something to take the sharp edge off their hunger. If she had her way the feast would come later, when the food had been dispensed with.

They ate their impromptu snack in the bedroom window seat, feeling deliciously decadent and romantic. They'd shed their clothing, which smelled of the barn, and chatted unselfconsciously in their skivvies. They laughed and the tiredness of the day slowly dissipated, leaving them lighthearted and relaxed.

They basked in warm visual embraces, often losing the thread of conversation as they gazed lovingly into each other's eyes. They reached out often to touch or caress each other, the temptation being much too great to resist.

Morgan didn't think he would ever get enough of her. It had been less than an hour since he'd last loved her but he knew he couldn't wait another hour to do so again. His desire for her was a palpable thing, a third presence in the room. Reluctantly he rose and went into the bathroom to warm up the abandoned bubble bath.

"Jolie," he called in an affected singsong. "Your bath and your knight await."

Jolie skimmed out of her champagne-colored silk teddy and let it fall in a heap at her feet. Wearing nothing but her smile, she opened the door and stepped brazenly into the bathroom.

"Did you want me?" she asked innocently.

"I did," Morgan answered huskily, allowing his eyes a quick, appreciative trip over her slim figure. "I do, and I always will."

He was already ensconced in the huge antique tub, and piles of frothy bubbles tickled his chin. He held out his hand, inviting her to join him.

"You're crazy."

His grin took her breath away. "That's right. I'm crazy for you."

She slipped into the opposite end of the tub. The warm, scented water caressed her as intimately as Morgan's heated gaze as she sank down into the bubbles. "Where's your rubber duck?"

He pointed to a wicker étagère across the room. "Still on the shelf. He gets lost in the bubbles."

Jolie spotted the toy and the source of all the heavenly bubbles at the same time. She laughed delightedly. "Mr. Bubble? That's what Meggie uses."

153

"Of course. Where do you think I heard about it? You didn't expect me to take a bubble bath in that flowery junk you women use, did you?"

"I never expected you to take a bubble bath at all, but here you are. You're the most surprising man, Morgan."

His gaze sobered. "Is that good or bad?"

Jolie laughed, full of happiness as she splashed him with a handful of water. "It's delightful. I wouldn't change a thing about you. You're absolutely perfect."

"No." Morgan sighed in mock depression. "I'm not perfect."

Jolie cleared away a mound of bubbles with both hands so she might scrutinize him completely. "Sorry, but you are definitely perfect. What is this alleged imperfection you claim to have?"

He raised his right foot out of the bubbles and manipulated the faucet at Jolie's side. Warm water ran into the tub. "My feet!" he said sadly. "Haven't you ever noticed how weird my toes are?"

Jolie gently caressed his foot, running her fingertips over the first three toes, which were all the same length, then over the two much shorter little ones. With his other agile foot Morgan turned off the water.

"Your feet have character." She massaged them lovingly. "And according to a comedian I saw on television, you're aquadextrous. Not everyone can operate faucets like that." She playfully nipped his little toe with her teeth. "Your feet are like the rest of you—oddball and adorable. I adore your feet."

Morgan leaned back, closing his eyes for a second, then raised his left foot for her ministrations. "It must be love if you adore my feet."

Jolie rubbed his foot languorously, then slipped her hand up the long, wet length of his leg. She had a better idea and closed her hands around a more enticing part of him, eliciting a rumbling groan of pleasure.

"Don't start anything you can't finish," he warned.

"I wasn't planning to," she answered levelly. She stood up, mindless of the suds clinging to her, and boldly admired his magnificence as he stepped out of the tub.

"Come here, woman," he commanded softly.

She glided into his arms and he wrapped her in a big soft towel before picking her up and tossing her over one broad shoulder. She experienced a strange déjà vu when he dropped her, minus the towel, amid the fur throws on his bed. His lips found hers and he murmured a promise against her mouth. "I'm going to kiss you senseless."

He was as good as his word. His mouth took charge of hers with the deliberation that was characteristic of him. Jolie's response was instant and total. She wanted the kiss to last forever. It was so perfect it could have been plucked straight from her fantasies. It was a long-sought treasure, finally discovered.

He stretched out beside her, and the crush of her skin against his sent hot flames of longing deep within him. She breathed his name against his moist lips.

Jolie's senses swirled madly. Beneath her the sensuous feel of the fur competed with the silky caress of Morgan's mustache as he explored the heated landscape of her body with his lips. She matched his exploratory tasting and it grew ever more rapacious.

One by one her senses sprang to life, acquainting themselves with the ecstasy that was Morgan. His gently seductive fingers fondled her to blazing awareness of him, and only him. She gasped, a captive of desire.

His lovemaking was both tender and questing. He groaned his delight in pleasing her, in eliciting soft sighs and ragged gasps from her. She savored the tautness of his skin, the rediscovery of his sinewy muscles. She clutched his shoulders, pressing herself against the lean length of him. His arms tightened around her, fanning the flames. His hand caressed her intimately and need rumbled through her pulsing veins with wild white water ferocity.

155

Their bodies merged, filling her with the sweetest rush of rapture she ever hoped to know. Morgan expertly prolonged their pleasure until, fevered with enflamed passion, they were flung over the edge into paradise, the land of ultimate enchantment.

Jolie lay stretched out in sated abandon, fully aware of every delicious inch of the virile, warm form pressed against her. Full of happiness and total satisfaction, she danced her fingertips over his back.

He raised above her on his elbows, his eyes warmly aglow, and touched his lips to hers. "Jolie, I love you." There was such tenderness in his whisper that her eyes filled with tears.

"I love you too, Morgan."

He kissed the tear from her cheek. "But it doesn't make me feel like crying. What's wrong?"

"Nothing. Everything is so perfect it scares me."

"I know. I've never felt this intense about anyone or anything in my life as I do about you. Let's not be afraid of it. Let's embrace it, enjoy it and savor it."

"Yes. And hope it lasts forever."

"It will." Morgan didn't have a doubt about that. He and Jolie would always know the complete happiness they enjoyed at this moment. He would make it his life's work.

"How happy will we be, Morgan?" Jolie settled into the warm circle of his arms.

"So happy that it will disgust all our friends."

She grimaced. "How romantic. I've been thinking about children. I think I'd like us to have a baby."

Morgan's heart stopped for a long second. He hadn't brought up the subject of children since the day of Meggie's accident. Her announcement filled him with gladness because he recognized that it was far more than her commitment to a future pregnancy. It was symbolic of her acceptance of a shared lifetime together—he and Jolie and Meggie together.

Jolie poked him in the ribs. "Do you have any baby pictures?"

"I was afraid you'd get around to asking that."

"I want to see them. It'll give me an idea of how our babies will look." She gave him a little shove. "Go get them, please."

"First you have to swear that you won't change your mind about marrying me and having my children after you've seen them."

Jolie made a face. "Are they that bad?"

"Swear, Jolie."

"Damn," Jolie swore, and Morgan sauntered out of the room to get the requested pictures, unconcerned about his nudity.

When he returned, he unceremoniously dumped a photo album on the bed beside her.

"Only one album?" she asked as she turned to the first page. "And you an only child?"

"Just one for now. After we're married and I feel more secure, I'll show you all of them."

Jolie fell in love all over again as she gazed at the fat little cherub smiling at her from a fur rug. "You were beautiful."

"I was fat and bald." Morgan lay down behind her and reached over to turn the page. "I'm not too bad in that one—the clothes hid some of the fat."

A wide toothless grin smiled up from the page. Jolie hoped they had a little son exactly like him. "Yes," she agreed impishly. "But you were still bald."

Morgan moved closer and his hand spread over her abdomen possessively. "Turn the page. I'm wearing a hat in the next one."

Jolie laughed. A hat was all the baby Morgan was wearing, and it was about fifty sizes too large. "How adorable. You really were adorable."

"I was fat and bald," he reiterated, closing the book and turning her to face him. "I'm adorable now."

157

"You certainly lost all that baby fat." She gently stroked the muscles of his back, her hands straying down his lean hips as he lay across her. "I love you so much, Morgan."

Morgan kissed the tip of her nose. "You still love me, even after those pictures?"

"More than ever."

"That's a relief."

"Aren't you going to tell me you love me?" Her fingertips slid down his back to follow the swell of his buttocks.

"I showed you those pictures, didn't I?" His lips began a trail of nibbling kisses from her jaw to her ear. "I love you with every fiber of my being. I want to show you just how much."

"Please do." Jolie could hardly breathe, but she gloried in the wide, wet crush of his mouth against hers. They succumbed eagerly and frantically again to the velvet chains of their passion until they were sated. They were an intimate tangle of limbs and sheets, flushed and damp all over and exhilaratingly well loved.

When Jolie awoke it was just past dawn. She was as bare as the day she was born and felt utterly safe in Morgan's arms, her cheek resting on his shoulder.

Morgan wasn't asleep but his eyes were closed, and she couldn't resist the temptation to watch him in repose. His chest hair was a wiry blond mat stretching up over his heart, then circling his navel and turning darker below. His shoulders were golden brown, his ribs strong and well molded, his stomach flat and hard. His thighs were pillars of muscle, and when the whole picture was put together the only word that came to her mind was *man*. Her man.

"Morgan?"

"Hmmm?"

"What are we going to do today? I need to call Sharon so I can pick up Meggie."

He leaned over her. The pads of his thumbs caressed

her cheeks; the weight of his chest crushed her breasts. He planted one heavy thigh between hers, pinning her beneath him. "Need I say more?" he asked in his rusty, sexy morning voice.

CHAPTER ELEVEN

An ineffable sense of dread swept through Jolie when she spotted the sleek black Lincoln with Texas plates parked in her narrow drive.

"Looks like you've got company, Jolie," Morgan said, aware of her terrible stillness.

"I don't have company," she said in a hollow voice. "I have trouble."

Morgan turned off the ignition and took her hand in his. "Whatever comes—whatever this is all about—know that I'm with you." He was prepared to battle whoever or whatever had put that cornered doe look back into her eyes.

Jolie squeezed his hand to let him know that she needed him with her, needed his support when she faced Mr. and Mrs. Winslow J. Meredith of Dallas.

Stephen's parents had gotten out of their car and were standing beside it by the time Jolie and Morgan reached them.

"Hello, Jolie," Larraine Meredith said tentatively. "It's so good to see you again." She looked nervously at her husband, as though he'd missed his rehearsed cue.

"Hello, Larraine. Winslow. You are the last two people on earth I expected to see this morning." Jolie hoped her honesty would set the tone for the confrontation that was sure to come.

Her ex-father-in-law looked disconcerted, but Jolie

knew it would take more than candor to get the upper hand with a petroleum czar who regularly faced leaders of countries and corporations without qualms.

It had been over three years since she'd heard from them, since they'd tried to relieve Stephen of his parental obligations with their money. What did they want? Why had they shown up today to spoil the utter happiness she had found at last with Morgan?

"Well?" Jolie asked the handsome, well-dressed couple. "You must be here for a reason, but I can't begin to guess what it is." Morgan recognized the false bravado in her words. She was scared to death, but from the way she squeezed his hand, he guessed she needed to put up a tough front for her unwelcome visitors.

"Could we talk, Jolie?" Mr. Meredith asked gently. "We'd like very much to talk with you."

Morgan took that opportunity to introduce himself and led the way inside, as Jolie seemed incapable of social amenities. He knew the older couple would prefer that he get lost so they could speak to Jolie in privacy, but Morgan resolved to stay. If push came to shove, he wanted them to know that he was on Jolie's side.

She stopped to pick up the folded piece of paper that had been dropped in her mail slot. She breathed easier when she read the short note. Sharon had taken Meggie out to breakfast at the local pancake house. They'd be back soon, but with any luck the Merediths would be gone before then. She didn't want to have to explain the sudden appearance of grandparents Meggie had never known existed.

"Why don't I make us all some coffee?" Morgan slipped into the kitchen, hoping that his temporary absence would start the conversational ball rolling. Jolie was perched on the edge of her chair like a nervous bird tensed for flight. The Merediths had resorted to throat clearing and nervous sighing to fill the silence.

Jolie would be damned if she would ask them again

161

what they were doing in her home. She wasn't going to make it easy for them and she had no intention of being gracious. They'd given up their right to courteous treatment long ago when they'd abandoned their granddaughter.

"We've been looking for you ever since we saw a story on the Dallas news," Meredith began.

"Yes, on the news," his wife echoed.

"What story?"

"About Meggie being lost. At some kind of fair?"

Comprehension was slow to dawn. Then Jolie recalled the young reporter and the story she'd filmed for the Oklahoma City news. "But that was a local story. Why was it shown in Dallas?"

"I suppose one of the wire services picked it up. It was on for just a moment. We almost missed it," Winslow Meredith said intently. "Both of us recognized you and I called someone I knew at the television station and got hold of the film. We've been searching for the two of you ever since."

"Ever since," Larraine repeated. "Your telephone number is unlisted and we didn't know if you were in Oklahoma City or one of the surrounding towns," she ended lamely.

"So you found us." Jolie's head jerked up, and she looked them right in the eye in a last-ditch effort to appear calm and courageous and cold. "That doesn't explain why you're here."

"We'd like to meet our granddaughter," Winslow stated matter-of-factly.

Jolie struggled to tamp down the hysteria that threatened. Had they come to try to take Meggie away from her? After denying their relationship for so long? The Merediths were used to getting what they wanted, but this time they were out of luck. Realizing that emotional displays would get her nowhere, she struggled to keep her voice calm.

162

"Your granddaughter?" She could be just as unfeeling as the Merediths.

"Yes. Meggie," Larraine said the name as if she adored the very sound of it. "We'd like to see little Meggie." Then the older woman took a handkerchief from her bag and sniffed delicately.

"I don't understand this sudden display of familial interest. You didn't visit her when she lived a few miles from you, so why drive all the way up here to see her now?" Jolie realized that she'd bared her claws again and that harsh words wouldn't change a thing. She tried another tack. "Look, Meggie and I have worked hard for the progress she's made and I don't want anything to interfere with that."

"We don't want that either." Winslow cleared his throat and accepted the cup of coffee Morgan offered him. "Look, Jolie, you have every right to be angry and bitter. You have every right to tell us to get the hell out of your house and never come back."

Jolie swallowed hard, wanting to do just that. But something she couldn't put a name to held her back.

"We only ask that you hear us out," he continued. "We've come here to ask your forgiveness. And to admit how very wrong we've been."

"Please, Jolie," Larraine piped up. "We've been so wrong. I hope you can find it in your heart to forgive us."

The woman was still living in Winslow's shadow, Jolie noted, still voicing his opinions instead of forming her own. Jolie remembered the last time she'd seen her former mother-in-law. Just after Jolie's own mother had died, Larraine had come to pay her respects. She had asked to hold the infant Meggie, and Jolie recalled that Larraine had shed a few tears that day. Somehow she'd known that Larraine had come without her husband's knowledge, and that small act of defiance had touched her.

So Winslow Meredith was ready to beg her forgive-

163

ness. That was a departure from the man she'd known before. He'd coldly accepted Stephen's lies and refuted Jolie's side of the story. There'd been no discussion offered then. Winslow J. Meredith subscribed to the never-explain, never-apologize school of thought.

"Does Stephen know you're here?" Jolie asked.

"No. We felt he didn't need to know. For now."

She searched the faces of the couple, looking for signs of their true intentions. She noticed a few more wrinkles, a few more stress lines. And she noticed their brimming eyes.

Jolie sighed. "All right. I'll hear you out."

Morgan sat quietly throughout the Merediths' story, holding Jolie's hand, trying to lend her some of his strength. What he heard tore at his heart, both for the bewildered couple and for Jolie, but most of all for Meggie. That the sweet little girl could have been so callously discounted by her own father made him sad and angry. He hoped he never met Stephen Meredith. He feared for the jerk's well-being if he did.

The Merediths, as they explained, had been caught in the middle, wanting to believe Jolie, wanting to acknowledge their grandchild, but having to accept the word of their only son. They had gone along with him because it was the path of least resistance and they had a social facade and a corporate unity to protect. And because they felt they had to.

"There had never been any history of deafness or other infirmities in our family, you see," the timid older woman pointed out. "How could our grandchild be deaf? We couldn't understand how such a thing could happen to us."

"It didn't happen to you." Jolie's voice had a cutting edge of bitterness to it. "But I see your point. You were so worried about what your precious friends would think —about how it would look for the Meredith family to harbor a 'defective' child." Painful memories threatened to overwhelm her. "You did everything except pin a scarlet letter on me."

"We were thoughtless and cruel. Selfish. We admit it. We just want your forgiveness so we can see the child. Please."

Morgan felt that Winslow's request was genuine, his shame obvious. But his words only made Jolie adopt an even fiercer version of her old fighting stance. It appeared she wasn't about to let them off that easily. The Merediths might be rich and powerful but they hadn't reckoned on Jolie's loyalty to her child.

"So what does seeing Meggie on that news program have to do with anything? She's still deaf, and according to you, she's not even your relative."

Jolie almost regretted her condemnation, for Larraine paled as though she'd been slapped.

The woman said with a sob, "Of course she's our grandchild. We were wrong to listen to Stephen."

Winslow looked levelly at Jolie and admitted his knowledge of Stephen's dissolute life. "Our son has been a big disappointment to us. It's taken a while but we've learned not to believe his lies."

This uncharacteristic admission grabbed at Jolie's heart. She knew what those words must have cost the man.

Larraine was now crying softly, her handkerchief pressed into service. "When we saw Meggie on that film, our hearts just went out to her. She looked so beautiful . . . just like a little angel. She seemed so precious and real to us."

"Meggie is real," Jolie proclaimed in a shaky voice, her emotions roiling and tumbling. She felt sick to her stomach—and at heart. She wanted to go back and start the day over—without the appearance of the Merediths.

During the past few years it had been easy to tell herself she hated them, but it was harder now with them sitting here looking old and lonely and lost. She'd held on to the anger, the bitterness, the betrayal for so long, she wasn't sure she wanted to let it go—even if it was possible. But what freedom there would be in ridding herself of the burden, of starting over with a clean slate!

"Please don't misinterpret our meaning. We want to be her grandparents—nothing more, nothing less."

"I don't know," Jolie said quietly. "I don't know what to think about any of this. It's very difficult to believe that you just happened to see her picture on television and now you've decided to love her. A change of heart like that is unlikely, and"—Jolie sighed, then added—"you'll have to excuse me if I find it hard to swallow."

"We really can't blame you for that. And we don't expect you to give us an answer today. All we ask is that you think about it for a while." Larraine dabbed at her tear-filled eyes.

"I'll try. That's all I can promise you." Jolie's past had come back to haunt her and she refused to cope with her warring emotions as her enemies witnessed the battle. She stood and walked to the door with a calmness and grace she didn't feel. She turned the knob, expecting her unwanted guests to make a hasty exit.

Instead a small curly-haired dynamo burst into the room.

"Mommy. Aunt Shar and Meggie eat stawbooey waffles." She stopped short when she saw the strangers in the room and stared at them with childish interest, her kitten clutched in her arms.

"Oh, Jolie," Sharon apologized breathlessly. "I tried to catch her before she ran in but . . ."

"It's all right. They were just about to leave anyway." She looked at the Merediths expectantly.

Meggie approached the couple on the couch and plopped down between them. "See my kitty. Her name Daisy. Pet her you." She thrust out the limp animal for Larraine to pet. "Feel her hum." Meggie took the other woman's hand and placed it against the kitten's chest, which vibrated with an audible purr. "That how Daisy talk to Meggie." She tilted her head and smiled her guaranteed-to-melt-the-heart-of-a-statue smile.

Larraine Meredith's eyes swam with unshed tears as she gazed pleadingly at Jolie over Meggie's head. Jolie knew what she was asking. She wanted permission to love her granddaughter, but at this moment Jolie couldn't find it in her heart to grant it.

They were begging her to share Meggie with them. Now—at this late date. Meggie had been hers and hers alone for so long. It had always been Meggie and Jolie, alone against all others. It was their way of life, the only way they knew. Yet the Merediths expected to walk into their lives as though nothing had ever happened. Meggie didn't need them; she had Jolie.

"She talks very well," Winslow was saying. "You've done a wonderful job with her, Jolie. I had no idea that she would be able to communicate so well." Remorse was evident in his words.

"Yes, she does." And if he had not been so quick to abandon his granddaughter, he would have known, Jolie thought as she crossed the room and plucked her daughter away from them. "Sharon, do you think you could take Meggie to the park for a while?"

"Why, sure. I guess so. How about it, Muffin?" Sharon asked, holding out her arms to Meggie. "Want to go to the park for a little while?"

"Daisy go."

"Of course."

It was obvious to Morgan that Jolie had no plans to introduce the Merediths to either Meggie or Sharon, who hesitated for just a moment at the door before finally departing. He was shocked by Jolie's rudeness, but he chalked it up to the surprise visit.

She'd been thrown off balance. But her apparent lack of clemency stunned him. He realized with sudden clarity that when it came to Meggie, Jolie could never be generous. She would never be willing to share her daughter with anyone—even him.

Winslow patted his wife's quaking shoulders as they prepared to leave. Jolie steeled her heart and pleaded silently for their quick departure. She didn't know how much longer she could hold back the racking sobs that threatened.

She wasn't sure of the exact reasons she felt like crying. For herself and the painful emotions she'd kept bottled up inside for so long? For Meggie, who'd been denied the delight of having grandparents, of feeling herself part of a family? For the Merediths, who had missed so much of Meggie's life already?

The Winslows left self-consciously, saying good-bye to Morgan and sending Jolie beseeching glances. As she stepped off the porch, Larraine turned and tried one last appeal.

"Please let us see Meggie. Let us be her grandparents at last."

"I can't do that. Not right now." Jolie looked away, her heart heavy with regret and pity. "I'm not sure I'll ever be able to."

"Won't you at least think about it?" Winslow entreated.

"I'll try," she said softly, striving to hide her emotion.

The raw hopefulness on the older man's face was painful to witness, and Morgan added, "I'm sure she'll give your requests her careful consideration."

Jolie glared at Morgan. Whose side was he on?

Meredith handed her a card. "If you change your mind, at any time, please call."

"I don't need the card." She hadn't forgotten their number. Maybe it wasn't fair to Meggie to deny her a chance to know her grandparents, and Jolie was willing to admit it. But being willing to forgive and being able to forgive were two very different things. "I've had over four years to think of little else—"

168

"Now, Jolie," Morgan warned. "Don't say anything you'll regret."

"Stay out of this, Morgan." It seemed to Jolie that Morgan had cast her as the villain in this plot, and she just couldn't handle that today.

Larraine Meredith clutched her purse to her chest and hurried to the car. Winslow faced Jolie and didn't try to hide his pain. "Is there anything—anything—we can do for you or Meggie? Is there anything you need?"

Jolie stiffened, angry at the Merediths all over again. How like the man to offer money, the balm for everything. She hadn't taken a penny from him years ago. What made him think she would want anything from him now? She glared at him, not trusting herself to answer. He slumped and walked away.

The powerful car soon disappeared from view. Jolie turned to Morgan and read the disappointment in his eyes. Had he expected her to act differently? He took her hand, but she yanked it from him and wheeled into the house.

Morgan stood on the porch for a few minutes after Jolie had gone inside and slammed the door. He tried to think through the scene that had just played itself out but could come to no satisfying conclusion about Jolie's behavior. They needed to talk.

He found her at the sink, furiously scrubbing coffee cups. She didn't turn when he came in but began drying the dishes and stacking them with a dangerous clatter in the cupboard.

"Go ahead," she dared him. "Say it."

"Say what?" He could tell from her tone that she was in no mood for talking and he quickly decided to postpone it. He poured himself a cup of coffee and sat down at the table.

"Whatever it is that you're finding so difficult to spit out," she goaded, turning to face him, one hand defiantly

169

planted on her hip. "Tell me how cruel and heartless you think I am."

"I never said that," he denied quietly. He reminded himself that Jolie was emotionally charged right now and he refused to let her pick a fight with him.

"You were thinking it," she accused, throwing her dishtowel at the table suspiciously close to where Morgan sat.

"You're not cruel or heartless, Jolie," Morgan said, taking a deep breath before plunging in. "But I don't think you were entirely fair to that old couple."

She rounded on him instantly. "Well, that's just fine. I wasn't fair to them. I suppose you think they were fair to Meggie and me?"

"No, I didn't say that. I think they were wrong, but it's obvious they've suffered a great deal from their mistake. They just want a chance to know their grandchild. Apparently, from what Meredith says, she may be the only one they'll ever have."

Jolie knew that Morgan was referring to Winslow's condemnation of his son's life-style, of his casual liaisons with women, of his inability to make commitments. There would probably be no other heirs for the Merediths.

"They can't have Meggie." How could Morgan think she'd allow them to contaminate her daughter with the spoils of their wealth? Why hadn't Morgan taken up for her? Why couldn't he see her side of this?

"Just like that? Sorry, but you had your chance and you blew it? Jolie, I never thought you would be so unforgiving, or so selfish."

"Selfish?" Spots of color surged into her vision. She felt betrayal and frustration. "Those people invented selfish. They are the most self-serving individuals you will ever meet, with the possible exception of their son."

"Maybe. But I felt sorry for them. And I feel sorry for

170

Meggie. You're denying her the only family she has, just to spite her father."

"You don't know what you're talking about." Jolie ground out the words. "You don't know anything about it at all."

"Then tell me," Morgan said gently. "Make me understand."

Jolie was loaded for bear, primed for a shouting match, but Morgan's softly spoken request stopped her short. Before she answered she tried to get her confused thoughts in order.

She *had* considered giving the Merediths the thread of hope they'd sought. That is, until Morgan had made her so mad. What was his motivation? Was he really just being an objective observer? Making objective assumptions? Or was his desire to see Meggie reconciled with the Merediths prompted by something else?

"You just want to get rid of Meggie," she accused, thinking he wasn't so different from other men after all.

Morgan was shocked by her accusation. "What?" he asked incredulously. "How can you say that?"

"Because if I let her grandparents have a part in her life, a say in her upbringing, then that will be less burden on you. You said you wanted to adopt Meggie, to love her as your own, but it seems to me that you're much too eager to hand her over to the Merediths."

"Jolie, that isn't true. I wasn't suggesting that you pack her clothes and send her off to Texas," Morgan denied softly. That Jolie should doubt his loyalty and his love for both of them hurt Morgan more than any pain he'd ever known. "And I think you know it. I love you. I love Meggie. I want what's best for her. I just happen to think she has the right to get acquainted with her natural grandparents."

"She isn't your child. You have no right to make decisions about her future. How could you possibly presume to know what's best for her?"

171

Her words bit coldly through Morgan's heart. "You're right." His voice was taut, his eyes sad. "She isn't my child. Because you won't allow it. You'll never give up a bit of your total control. That's what this is really all about. You're afraid to let her love anyone else. You're afraid of losing her total love."

Jolie said nothing, but he could see the denial forming on her lips. Before she could speak, he continued. "I won't settle for less than equality, Jolie. If we marry, I want to be an equal partner in the rearing of both Meggie and any children we might have. I don't want to be one of those absentee fathers who check in once in a while to hand out treats and offer a weekly piggyback ride. I want to share everything. Completely."

Jolie hung her head and tried to fight the tears that were already forming. "I'm sorry, Morgan. I understand how you feel. I really do. It's just that I'm so mixed up. I'm so confused by everything. It's all happened so suddenly—you, us, the Merediths, everything. I need time to think. I need more space."

He went to her and drew her into the circle of his arms. He stroked her hair and brushed the top of her head with his lips. "I'm sorry, love, that you had to go through this today. But in a way I'm glad it happened. It opened my eyes to something that would have become an issue between us sooner or later."

"What's that?"

"That you don't trust me enough to share your child with me. That you aren't willing to let me have a say in decisions affecting our future. You know, it's really nothing to me whether Meggie ever sees her grandparents or not. Maybe they don't deserve to know her; I don't know. All I know is that I have to decide if I can live with your attitudes. I won't try to change you; that's no basis for a relationship. But until you give up the past, I just don't think you're ready for the future."

Morgan set her from him. "I'm going now. Not forever

172

—just until we've both had time to think things through."

Jolie saw the tears in his eyes, but he blinked them back. "Oh, Morgan. Things just happened too fast for us. I've spent years getting my life back in order. You can't expect me to change overnight. I guess there's no such thing as once upon a time with a fairy tale ending, or knights in shining armor. Maybe there's only reality and toads."

"Maybe," Morgan said softly, regretfully. "But I believe in once upon a dream. I think that's what we've had."

"We didn't have a courtship, or the getting-to-know-you period that is so important. We were so caught up in the dreamlike magic of our discoveries that we didn't reckon on all the dragons that might be lurking."

"I'll let it be your decision, Jolie. I know we can't marry under these circumstances, but I know, too, that we can work things out. Let me be your knight. Let me give you that fairy-tale beginning and help slay the dragons." He held her face gently in his hands. "Let me help you dream your dreams."

He kissed her, and both of them were charged with the bittersweet emotions of what might never be. "Morgan . . ."

"I'll be waiting for a sign."

Then he was gone, and Jolie didn't even try to stop him.

Jolie was still slumped on the couch when Sharon and Meggie returned from their outing. She relayed to her friend what had happened, expecting sympathy from that quarter.

"So it doesn't matter how much he loves you and Meggie?" Sharon asked with characteristic directness.

"Of course it matters. He made a valid point, but you don't understand. He doesn't have the big picture. He wasn't around when I was suffering so much because of Stephen."

"Oh." Sharon gave her an I-see-the-light look. "So you're punishing Morgan because he wasn't around to save you from Stephen."

"I'm not trying to punish anyone."

"Really? You could have fooled me. I think you've done a commendable job of punishing yourself for years."

"No, I haven't. It's just too difficult to trust again, to believe in a man. First my father, then Stephen. Even Stephen's parents just turned their backs on me when I needed their emotional support. I'm not sure I can ever forgive that."

"Maybe they did what they did out of love."

"Love? How can you even think that?"

"Should they love their son less because he isn't worthy? Do you plan to withhold your love from Meggie if she ever lies to you? Ever disappoints you? Maybe they wanted to believe him because it was too painful not to. I'd say they sacrificed a lot trying to keep their love intact."

"I don't know." Jolie rubbed her temples, trying to erase the image of the Merediths that Sharon's words had conjured. She couldn't get past the pain she'd seen in their faces when they looked at their grandchild. "When I saw them standing there today, all the old anger came pouring back. I'm not so sure they really deserve another chance."

"What about Meggie?" Sharon prodded.

"I don't know that either." Jolie felt hurt, confused and a little ashamed of her flint-hearted treatment of the older couple. She tried to feel justified but couldn't summon pride for her actions.

"So forget them. What's important is how you feel about sharing your life and your child with the man you love. You do love him, don't you?"

"Very much. But when he started talking about shar-

174

ing Meggie, about letting the Merediths back into our lives, I began to doubt his motives. I'm afraid I'll lose everything I've worked so hard to build."

"I'm not sure a wall around your heart is all that important, Jolie. Think about Meggie—doesn't she deserve a chance at a normal life? With not only a mother to love her but a father as well? Isn't she entitled to brothers and sisters and all the joy and misery that come with sibling relationships? Aren't you entitled to be happy? To be loved?"

Was she? Hadn't life taught her differently? Wasn't it Morgan's sudden and complete offer of commitment that scared her so? How could she ever live up to those idealistic expectations? "I don't know, Sharon; I just don't know."

Sharon stared at Jolie with amazement. "You don't know? How can you say such a thing? Of course you're entitled to happiness, and Morgan is offering it on a silver platter. Take a chance, Jolie. Don't settle for emptiness because you want to avoid pain."

Was that what she was doing? Already a sense of loss was filling the empty pockets of her spirit. Morgan had been gone only a few minutes, and she already missed him and wanted him back in her life. The pain she felt now was worse than any that had come before.

Jolie hugged her friend for putting into words all the free-floating thoughts tumbling around in her head. She wasn't sure she could accept Morgan's terms, but she knew she didn't want to lose him. She'd take the time he'd offered.

She could only hope her knight's biggest virtue was patience.

CHAPTER TWELVE

As the days wore on, Jolie tried several methods of coping with her loneliness. She tried concentrating on her work, but every time she walked through the tearoom she was reminded of the first day Morgan had been there. She was distracted by visions of him in a busboy's apron, laughing and teasing and making her feel alive. Work was no place to get over Morgan.

She tried to spend even more time with Meggie, but that was hardest of all. The little girl continually asked for Morgan, wanting to know when she could visit him and Tess, when she could see Georgia again. Even the kitten reminded Jolie of what she had given up.

One quiet Sunday afternoon Sharon dragged Jolie to the mall on a shopping trip, ostensibly to get her mind off Morgan, but in the very first shop they entered, Jolie found a tiny porcelain frog with bright blue eyes. She nearly blubbered like a baby as she made the purchase that now sat on her windowsill, silently exhorting her to throw off her fears and bring Morgan back into her life.

Meggie's fascination with Barbara Thompson's advancing pregnancy presented Jolie with an unexpected problem. "Why can't Meggie get sister or brother. Ryan is."

"You've got your kitten." Meggie hadn't cared for that answer, making it quite plain that Daisy was not an adequate substitute.

Without going too deeply into the facts of life, Jolie tried to explain that in order to have a baby there must be a father. She braced herself for the next question. She had long dreaded the day when Meggie would become perceptive enough to question the whereabouts of her own father. She couldn't lie to her child, but how could she tell the truth when the truth was so painful? She couldn't bear to see Meggie hurt as she herself had been hurt.

A parent's rejection was not an easy thing to cope with.

But Jolie had a reprieve. Meggie was not yet interested in learning about her own father, it seemed. "Morgan be daddy. Lucky baby," the little girl suggested logically.

It was almost as difficult to explain why that wouldn't be possible as it would have been to answer questions about Stephen.

Meggie couldn't accept the disappearance of Morgan from her life and seemed to lose some of the progress she had made. She moped around the house, lost some of her old sparkle and carried on lengthy one-way conversations with "my Morgan."

Jolie knew the child missed him as much as she did herself.

The overwhelming sense of being alone was far greater than what she had felt after her divorce. With a sick mother and an infant to care for, she had been constantly busy, but no amount of work had taken away her loneliness. She hadn't thought she could ever feel worse.

Until now. She longed for Morgan. Just thinking about him brought back memories that made her want to laugh and cry. What she had with him was better than anything she'd ever had before, and she felt the loss profoundly. It was worse knowing it was of her own making.

She spent her days sorting through her feelings, especially those concerning the Merediths. What would she have done in their place? Wouldn't her loyalty to her own child override her feelings for anyone else? She began to

177

understand for the first time. She had let her own bitterness cloud her good sense, and it was suddenly clear to her that pride and stubbornness were not worth the price she and Meggie would have to pay.

The first step in casting off the past would be learning forgiveness. She wasn't sure she could let go completely, not at first. She wouldn't be willing to allow the couple to take Meggie home with them for visits, and she wasn't ready to return to Dallas and the scene of so much pain.

But she could extend the hand of reconciliation and friendship to the Merediths. She could give Meggie back her family, and in doing so perhaps create an even closer bond between the two of them.

If she could make peace with the past, she could embrace the future. Morgan was her future.

Jolie reached for the telephone and punched in the area code for Dallas.

Morgan hadn't really expected it to take Jolie so long to reach a decision. Or maybe she had reached one and this silence was her answer. He couldn't accept the fact that he had lost her. He wasn't about to give up without a fight.

Many times he'd caught himself driving to her neighborhood, ready to force a confrontation. But he always turned back at the last minute. He'd promised her time, and time she would get—even if it killed him. Just as he'd used restraint in the early stages of their relationship, so would he use it now.

The stakes were too high to blow it all at this point.

On a Monday afternoon following a solitary weekend during which he'd done nothing but brood and imagine Jolie in every room of his house, he entered his office in the history building of the university and found a package on his desk. It was wrapped in plain brown paper and bore no return address.

He tore it open eagerly, hoping against hope.

178

His heart leapt when he unwrapped a tiny tissue-covered figurine. It was a silly-looking porcelain frog with bulging blue eyes. He read the enclosed card over and over again: "I kissed this frog—I'm waiting for him to turn into my Prince Charming." It was signed simply, "J."

Relief and joy surged through him, and the laugh that rumbled down the hallowed halls of the history department attracted a few curious stares.

He only had one more class for the day, and he found it difficult to concentrate. His mind was racing with plans for a quick but thorough courtship such as Ms. Jolie O'Day had never known.

Jolie kept glancing at the clock in her office. Surely Morgan had received the package by now. She'd sent it by a very reliable courier—one of his students who was a long-time customer of the tearoom. Why hadn't he called?

It was her habit to go to the bank each afternoon with the deposit, but she had put off leaving in the hope of hearing from Morgan. But when it looked as though he wouldn't be calling, she took the bank bag from the safe. Had she waited too long? Had he given up on her and changed his mind? Why had she been so foolish as to think anything was as important as their future together?

Filled with dread at the possibility, Jolie prepared to leave when the melodic strains of harmonizing voices reached her. She rose and peeked out into the dining room. A group of madrigal singers in full formal attire was stationed near the front window, their voices rising joyfully in an acapella arrangement of a fifteenth-century love song.

The surprised diners, many with forks poised mid-air, stopped to listen to the rollicking song. The choral group played up to their audience by smiling, winking and thoroughly enjoying themselves. At the end of the first num-

179

ber, the dining room vibrated with laughter and applause. One of the male singers raised his hand for silence before he spoke.

"The next song is dedicated to the lady Jolie O'Day, from her apprentice knight." Everyone looked at Jolie, and she blushed furiously despite herself. So this was his way of letting her know he'd gotten her message.

She smiled sheepishly, but her grin was soon replaced by open-mouthed astonishment as the little choir launched into a perfectly bawdy tribute to a shy, pink-cheeked milkmaid. The tearoom patrons roared their approval, but Jolie wasn't sure if she could maintain her composure through another ditty.

The final offering was a tender, lyrical love song. The words were full of enchantment, and the artful blending of male and female voices produced a haunting melody. When the song ended, the singers bowed and curtsied, taking their leave as abruptly as they'd arrived.

Jolie was amazed at how quickly Morgan had arranged for the impromptu serenade. She didn't know why she was surprised to discover he could work such magic. Surely she'd learned by now to expect the unexpected where he was concerned.

Sharon stepped up beside her. "What a man! And what an imagination! I've never heard of anything so romantic in my life," she gushed. "Gee. Sending your own personal balladeers to serenade your lover."

"I know," Jolie agreed dreamily. "He does have a flair for the unusual. But then he's an extraordinary man."

"I wonder what he's planning for an encore?"

Jolie smiled smugly. "I can't wait to find out."

On the way to the bank downtown, Jolie had time to reflect on Morgan's methods. Obviously he'd accepted the sign she sent him and was acting on it. He was turning their reconciliation into a memorable experience. What was she supposed to do next? Call him? Go to him? She decided to wait and see if he contacted her again.

She didn't have long to wait.

When she got out of the van, she glanced at the electronic sign atop the tall bank building. It seemed unseasonably warm, and she was curious about the temperature. She was willing to concede that it was possibly all those fond thoughts of Morgan that had warmed her so.

Instead of degrees Fahrenheit and Celsius, she was shocked to see her name blink across the billboard in five-foot-high letters. She watched the rest of the message with curiosity and a thrilling sense of elation, not to mention a bit of embarrassment.

J-O-L-I-E—I—L-O-V-E—Y-O-U—W-I-L-L—Y-O-U —B-E—M-Y—L-A-D-Y—F-O-R-E-V-E-R—???

He certainly wanted to make sure that everyone in Norman knew his intentions. First he'd sent a group of minstrels to her place of business and now he'd made her the object of a high-tech marriage proposal. If that was what it was. Couldn't he ever just do the normal thing, like calling her on the telephone or talking to her privately?

No, she answered, Morgan Asher would never do the expected. She wouldn't want him to. Wasn't that why she found him so fascinating? What was she letting herself in for if she agreed to spend forever with him?

Her face colored with memories of exactly what she'd be getting.

"So?" the young teller asked as soon as Jolie unzipped the bank bag and slid the deposit across the counter. "Are you going to marry him?"

"Marry who?" Jolie feigned innocence.

"Come on, Jolie. Don't I always let you know before Sharon's checks have a chance to bounce? There can't be another Jolie in Norman. The name isn't that common. I saw him when he came in to hire the billboard. It took him a while to convince Mr. Yates to allow anything so

181

personal. Usually it's just *happy birthday* or something like that, but I guess Mr. Yates is just an old softie when it comes to love."

The teller watched Jolie expectantly, but when no further information was forthcoming, the girl added, "Personally, I think the old guy kind of liked the idea of playing cupid. Your man looked like he could charm the birds right out of the trees, so I don't suppose Mr. Yates stood much of a chance. He's a real cutie."

"Mr. Yates?" Jolie asked nonchalantly.

"No," she said with a laugh. "Your fella. Mr. Tall Blond and Gorgeous."

"Yes, that sounds like him. I'm afraid to ask, but just how long is that electronic love letter going to flash its message to everybody this side of Mars?"

The girl didn't answer until she'd finished counting Jolie's change order. "Unfortunately," she said sadly, handing her the bag, "just for the rest of the day. A reporter from the *Transcript* has already been here making inquiries. I guess it's stirred up a bit of excitement."

"I guess. No one told the reporter who I am, did they?"

"Of course not," she said, astounded that Jolie would even ask. "We respected your privacy. Everyone's been talking about it. I think it's because no one ever really has enough romance in their lives. What do you think?"

"That's probably it," Jolie agreed, all the time thinking how lucky she was.

Jolie couldn't miss the amused glances she received as she left the bank, and she couldn't decide whether to laugh or cry. She'd always maintained the reputation of being a cool-headed businesswoman. She'd always been a very private person whose low-profile personal life was nothing if not discreet. Morgan had changed all that. Now she would be the topic of speculation and gossip. It was as if he'd brought the public in on the act to ensure that everyone understood his intentions were honorable.

Also, he'd made sure that she could not ignore his gestures.

Not that she wanted to. She missed him and she'd wasted too much time already—time they could have been together, time they could have been sharing with love and laughter. She would never really be whole again without Morgan. He was her other half. Why had he understood the kismet between them from the beginning while it had taken Jolie so much soul-searching to accept?

It didn't matter. What mattered was that they would be together soon. He'd call, or come to the tearoom. Or, better still, he'd be at her house when she got home. Then after they'd indulged in a long session of exquisite love-making, they would work out the irksome details of the rest of their lives. She longed to be swept back under Morgan's spell, to know once more the joy of the love they shared.

She attempted to work on her ledgers, but she was jumpy and tired from willing the telephone to ring. It was near closing time when Sharon entered her office with a long white florist's box.

"These just arrived." Grinning, she put the box down on Jolie's desk. "Prince Charming strikes again."

Jolie opened the gift and found two dozen perfect chocolate roses on long candy stems, nestled in green tissue. The enclosed card read simply "M," and Jolie was touched by the old-fashioned sentiment the gift conveyed. This feeling of being pursued, of being wooed, was new and delightful. She was being romantically courted by a master.

"Well, I've heard of sending candy and flowers, but these are the first candy flowers I've ever seen," Sharon commented.

"He's so—so romantic. As much as I enjoy seeing these offerings, I'd rather have him in person. I don't know what he'll do next and the suspense is killing me."

183

"Yeah," Sharon agreed. "But what a way to go. Say, why don't I pick up the Muffin and keep her occupied so you can go home and see if he's camping on your doorstep?"

"Oh, Sharon, you're wonderful. Thanks." Then Jolie recalled a commitment she'd made a week before. "Oh no, I can't. Meggie's invited to Ryan Thompson's birthday party tonight. I've got the gift right here in my desk drawer."

"No problem," Sharon assured. "I love parties where the guests run around acting barbaric, throwing food, upchucking on the rug. I went to plenty of them in college. Give me the gift and get out of here."

"You *are* wonderful!'

"Just go put that guy out of his misery."

Morgan's Chevy was not parked in her drive. She had so expected him to be there, it took a few moments before the fact registered. It was early; maybe he would call. Or come over later.

She went inside and leaned against the closed door. She'd have to make the next move. Was *that* what he was waiting for?

Daisy wound her lithe body around Jolie's ankles, purring and meowing. Jolie was so busy trying to frame her plan of action that she ignored the kitten's bid for attention. When she finally looked down she discovered a note that had been slipped under the door.

"Jolie, I want to marry you. And I promise to make you smile at least once a day. I'm in our special place." The note was signed, "Morgan."

Jolie held back the curtain of vines and pushed open the wooden gate. Her heart plummeted when she scanned the little glade and didn't see him there. Now that her mind was made up, she was irritated by the delay in giving him her answer. She stood among the

184

yawning and stretching shadows of twilight, filled with disappointment and uncertainty.

A much-loved voice called nonchalantly, "I'm so glad we're going to start meeting like this."

She spotted him then, reclining in the deep shade under one of the huge maples. She went to him, her pulse thudding with each step. Her love for him squeezed out everything else, and she was oblivious to the cricket chorus churring industriously from some hidden spot. She was barely conscious of the dewy grass that tickled her toes through her sandals and scarcely noticed the flicker of fireflies sewing sequins in the air.

He'd spread a patchwork quilt and was propped up on a mountain of pillows. Nearby was a tray of cheese, crackers and fruit. A bottle of wine was cooling in a silver bucket, and two thin-stemmed glasses balanced precariously on the quilt's bumpy landscape. This was the moment he'd waited for—the moment she could come to him unencumbered by ghosts from the past.

She stood over him, her glance taking in everything. She wanted to fling herself into his arms and stay there forever. When their eyes met and held, Jolie's problems evaporated and nothing seemed important enough to keep them apart any longer. "Expecting company?"

"Not anymore," Morgan said. He patted the quilt and with a glance urged her into a comfortable position beside him. "What do you think of our fairy-tale beginning so far?"

"Let's just say you got my attention. I'd like to hang around for the ending."

"Endings do not figure in my plans for our future. However, I do have some doozy surprises projected for our tenth, twenty-fifth and fiftieth anniversaries."

"I can hardly wait," she whispered, rushing into his arms. His quick embrace and the fierceness of his kiss told her he had waited with anything but patience. His mouth tasted of the night, and the sweet, fresh smell of dew clung to him. Her answering kiss was just as intense, her response to him just as fervent as his to her.

"You've always known, haven't you," she whispered against his warm lips. "You've always been sure that it would come to this."

Morgan wrapped his arms around her and drew her full-length against him. He raised himself onto one elbow and gazed into her upturned face. "I didn't doubt it for a moment. I always knew you were the one woman I could love for all time. That's why I was so hurt by your lack of confidence in me. That's why I knew I had to back away, giving you time to trust me.

"When I was a little boy there were woods behind our house. One day a young doe ventured into our yard and I was overcome by the beauty of the wild creature. My first impulse was to rush up to her, capture her in some way, to prevent her from running away.

"My father knew better. He convinced me that the only way she would ever learn to trust me was if I took things slowly and didn't frighten her. He taught me to stand still, to learn patience, to give the doe a chance to get used to my scent and my presence.

"Little by little, day after day, I approached her when she appeared. It took a long time, but finally she let me walk right up to her and gently stroke her soft hide. I'll never forget the exhilaration I felt that day."

Jolie snuggled closer to him, running her hands over the wide expanse of his chest. "I love you, Morgan. I'm glad you waited."

"I love you, too, Jolie. You *and* Meggie. When I think how I nearly lost you both by charging in and demanding your trust, I get scared. Losing both of you would be more than I could stand. You reminded me of that frightened little deer the day the Merediths came to call. I knew I would have to let you come to me."

"I'm sorry it took me so long, but I had to be sure of what I wanted. I had to be certain that whatever decision

186

I made concerning the future would be the right one. I found out you were right about a lot of things."

"Like what?"

"Like clinging to old hurts that were keeping me from opening up to new happiness. I guess I was guilty of destroying the flowers in my fury at the weeds."

"Almost guilty. Have you finally worked it all out?" Morgan tightened his hold on her. He wouldn't let her leave him again, but he didn't want any shadows clouding their life together.

"Yes. I've missed you so much. Meggie talks about you constantly and has even nominated you as a possible candidate to provide her with a baby brother."

He laughed. "I always said that kid was smart. How about her mother? Do I get her vote as well?"

"Oh, yes. You were right about the expansive qualities of love. By loving you and the children we'll have together, I'll only have more love to give Meggie. And she'll have more people to love as well. She'll have a chance at a normal life and she'll have a father she can be proud of."

Morgan's lips found the pulse at her neck. His heart swelled with his love for her and the words she had used to express her own. She really was ready to let him in. His only regret was that she hadn't found the strength to pardon the Merediths. He hoped that in time she would come around to a new way of thinking about her ex-in-laws.

"So everything is going to work out after all. You get me to slay your dragons, I get you to turn my castle into a home, Georgia gets an instant grandchild with the promise of more. And Meggie gets a grandmother to play with."

Jolie smiled up at him, her eyes filled with the joy she felt. "I just hope she doesn't get too spoiled by all the attention she's bound to get from so many grandparents."

187

Morgan's brow arched in question, and Jolie explained. "I spoke to Winslow and Larraine. I warned them that I wasn't ready to welcome them with open arms yet, but I was willing to give it a chance."

Morgan enfolded her in an emotional hug. He understood what it had cost her to take the first tentative step toward forgiveness. "You won't regret it."

"You know, it's funny, but I don't think I will. It won't be easy. I still have reservations and maybe always will have. But I plunged in and invited them up for dinner next Sunday. I hope Meggie won't be too overwhelmed by having so much sprung on her all at once." Her glance found him smiling the rakish smile that had first stolen her heart. "Will you be there too? I'd feel better if you—"

"Shh-h-h." He placed a fingertip on her lips. "I'll be there. Where else do I belong?"

"Oh, Morgan . . ."

"Quiet. There's a time for talking and a time for . . ." He paused to nuzzle her neck.

"Not talking?" Jolie supplied breathlessly.

"Exactly." He stroked her hair and rained a shower of kisses on her face. He murmured sweet promises, and Jolie didn't doubt for one moment that they would all be kept.

Now you can reserve June's
Candlelights
before they're published!

♥ You'll have copies set aside for *you*
   the instant they come off press.
♥ You'll save yourself precious shopping
   time by arranging for *home delivery.*
♥ You'll feel proud and efficient about
   organizing a system that *guarantees* delivery.
♥ You'll avoid the disappointment of not
   finding *every* title you want and need.

ECSTASY SUPREMES $2.75 each

☐ 173 **A PERILOUS AFFAIR,** Linda Randall Wisdom . . 16868-6
☐ 174 **DOUBLE MASQUERADE,** Alison Tyler 12120-5
☐ 175 **CALLAHAN'S GOLD,** Tate McKenna 11076-9
☐ 176 **SUMMER OF PROMISES,** Barbara Andrews . . . 18411-8

ECSTASY ROMANCES $2.25 each

☐ 510 **THE VIXEN'S KISS,** Jackie Black 19342-7
☐ 511 **THE BEST REVENGE,** Edith Delatush 10483-1
☐ 512 **SIREN FROM THE SEA,** Heather Graham 18057-0
☐ 513 **DECEPTION AND DESIRE,** Suzannah Davis . . . 11754-2
☐ 514 **CLEO'S TREASURE,** Rose Marie Ferris 11294-X
☐ 515 **FORBIDDEN PASSION,** Marilyn Cunningham . . 12660-6
☐ 49 *ELOQUENT SILENCE, Rachel Ryan* 12106-X
☐ 51 *ALL'S FAIR, Anne N. Reisser* 10098-4